INDIAN RAID

When Dave Watson, accompanied by Marcus Haverstraw, Buffalo Bill Cody, and Wild Bill Hickock, arrived at the Stearns ranch, the autumn moon hung low overhead. The night was crisp and clear, and even at first sight the riders could tell that the place had been attacked and put to the torch. Bodies littered the ground—the carcasses of horses and cattle, and the twisted forms of men, both whites and Plains Indians.

They dismounted and scoured the ruins, searching for the body of Deanna MacPartland. But there were no signs of any female presence in the charred remains of the Stearns ranch, though the Kansan did come upon something he recognized.

He peered down at the bloody bundle of flesh, bone and ragged, seared clothing. "John Hartung," the Kansan said quietly, causing Marcus Haverstraw to gasp at the name of Deanna MacPartland's abductor. "Took me a while to recognize him without his scalp."

"You know what happened to Deanna, Dave?" Bill Cody asked.

"What happened to 'er, Bill?" the Kansan asked in turn.

"Looks like the Cheyenne got 'er," Bill Cody told him simply.

"That means she'll stay alive," Dave said hopefully. "I got to git 'er back, boys," he told his friends at last.

THE KANSAN SERIES

#1	SHOWDOWN AT HELL'S CANYON	LB 774
#2	ACROSS THE HIGH SIERRA	LB 820
#3	RED APACHE SUN	LB 877
#4	JUDGE COLT	LB 937
#5	WARM FLESH, HOT LEAD	LB 978
#6	LONG HARD RIDE	LB 989
#7	TRAIL OF DESIRE	LB 1017
#8	SHOOT-OUT AT THE GOLDEN SLIPPER	LB 1044

KANSAN #9

THE CHEYENNE'S WOMAN

Robert E. Mills

LEISURE BOOKS NEW YORK CITY

A LEISURE BOOK

Published by

Dorchester Publishing Co., Inc.
41 E. 60 St.
New York City

Copyright © 1983 by Dorchester Publishing Co., Inc.

All rights reserved. No part of this book may be reproduced or transmitted in any form or by any electronic or mechanical means, including photocopying, recording or by any information storage and retrieval system, without the written permission of the Publisher, except where permitted by law.

Printed in the United States of America

PROLOGUE

THE CHEYENNE'S WOMAN

The campfire flared suddenly as one of the band of Indians who sat around it threw in a pile of buffalo chips, and the white smoke spiralled up to the stars, its vanishing wisps caught in the hard, cold light of the autumn moon. The air was chill and crisp, and the absence of wind accentuated the sounds of the night. Winter was not far off, and the teeming life of the Great Plains had begun to reflect the seasonal change, as birds and animals commenced their migrations or went into hibernation. Soon, biting winds would scour the plains, and the northers, those sudden, unexpected blizzards, would force even the nomadic tribes of Indians into their winter quarters, seeking shelter in camps whose natural advantages included a source of water and protection from the knifing winds.

Twenty-two braves sat around the campfire that night, their blankets wrapped around their lean, sinewy bodies as they smoked and gazed into the dancing flames. They were a mixed lot, a band whose members were drawn from more than one tribe. The majority of the braves were Cheyenne, led by a tall young buck named Grey Thunder. With them were six Sioux and three Arapaho braves, Indians whose tribes had long been the close allies of the Cheyenne. The band sat out under the stars on the prairie of northeastern Colorado, where they had come to hunt the buffalo who would soon cross that place in the course of their migrations.

The camp of this particular band, where the hunters sat and discussed their plans for the morning's hunt, was not a large one. In it were several women, and the ever-present dogs that stalked the camps. The dogs were used by the Indians as pack animals, and pulled the travois of the tribes as they pursued their nomadic way of life across the plains. And in one of the teepees was a white woman.

This was not a regular Cheyenne encampment, nor was it the regular quarters of the Sioux or Arapaho. This was a renegade band, and it received no aid or comfort from either Indian nor white man. Grey Thunder had killed a man when he had been drinking the white man's fire-water; he had killed another Cheyenne. That was a great crime among his people, and so they had banished Grey Thunder from their midst. His family was under the same stigma. Though they were able to remain with the tribe, they were no longer numbered among the Cheyenne during the great magical ceremonies such as the Sacred Arrow Renewal and the Sun Dance.

Grey Thunder ranged the plains under the cloud of his exile and dishonor. But his pride and hope were not lost to him, for it was the custom of his people to rehabilitate their criminals, and someday he knew that the tribe's collective wisdom and mercy would enable him once more to rejoin them. At that time, he would come with a great offering of horses to the peace chief, and beg for readmittance to the tribe. And if that old worthy felt Grey Thunder had learned his lesson and would henceforth unswervingly follow the Way of the Cheyenne, all would be well, and the murderer, his guilt expiated by his long exile and his family's dishonor, would be granted a fresh start in life.

That was the vision of redemption which the leader of the renegade band held in his heart, but its actualization was still years away. Grey Thunder was condemned to many more moons of wandering and exile. He had been joined in his course by several of his young male relatives and a number of other outcasts from the other Cheyenne tribes. The Sioux and Arapaho braves were young men as well, for Grey Thunder was a mighty warrior, and even in exile his renown called out to the wilder and more adventurous of his tribesmen and their allies. So it was that the band was formed, and Grey Thunder led it over the southern plains, hunting the buffalo and terrorizing the hated white—attacking small, isolated settlements and plundering them for food, weapons and ammunition, as well as ambushing the occasional stagecoach or wagon train.

Anger and vengeance were in the air, ever since the whites had violated the Treaty of Medicine Lodge, and the hotter heads among the tribes of the plains counselled war. The United States Cavalry, woefully understaffed since the end of the War between the States, had its hands full patrolling an area nearly the size of the continent of Europe. Tempers flared and rapidly soared to the boiling point, with no prospect of reconciliation in sight, and the only force strong enough to cool things down was the winter itself. But the winter had not yet set in. . . .

Grey Thunder handed the pipe to the man on his left, his younger brother, Running Antelope. "I am going to my teepee now," he grunted, rising with the swiftness and agility of a mountain lion.

"My brother goes to sleep early these nights," was Running Antelope's wry comment, and one which caused the other braves seated around the campfire to smile among themselves.

"That is because he has much to do before morning," one of the Sioux, a big man named Tall Elk, deadpanned as Grey Thunder walked out of the circle of light and into the darkness that lay just beyond it. Somewhere in the distance, to the south, toward Mexico, a coyote howled.

The other Indians in the circle all nodded, much amused by the true nature of Grey Thunder's departure and the ironical commentary which had accompanied the Cheyenne's parting statement. "It is not the buffalo that my brother has gone after this time," said Running Antelope as he accepted the pipe from a young brave known as Track of the Lightning. The latter had received this name on account of the white streak in his hair that had been with him practically since birth.

"Golden Woman is very beautiful," Track of the Lightning commented, beginning to puff on the pipe.

"She is very beautiful," Running Antelope repeated as Track of the Lightning passed the pipe to a scar-faced Sioux known as Buffalo Hump. "And I hope she will not bring bad luck to us."

The small fire in Grey Thunder's tent was burning low as the Cheyenne entered, its flickering light fitfully illuminating the objects within. At the far end of the teepee a form lay wrapped in an old blanket whose faded red and blue stripes were smudged with the grey ashes of the fire. Beneath the recumbent form was a buffalo robe, which kept it from the packed earth that was the teepee floor.

As Grey Thunder let go of the tent flap, the figure sat up and stared across the fire at him, eyes blinking in an attempt to adjust to the darkness of the teepee.

"I have come back," said Grey Thunder in a low voice, as he moved noiselessly toward the woman in the blanket, walking around the outer rim of the circle described by the shape of the structure.

The woman nodded as the Cheyenne came around the teepee, a lock of bright blonde hair falling down over her smooth, high forehead. Her eyes were blue as prairie flowers, and the light of the flickering fire danced in them as she looked up at the brave, who now stood before her. Her skin was pale and smooth and soft to the touch, and the Cheyenne warrior nodded approvingly as he reached out a hand and stroked her face.

A moment later he was down on the buffalo robe, kneeling beside her, naked except for the breechclout that covered his loins. "Your skin is as smooth as the windswept stone of the bluffs that face the river," he said in Cheyenne as his brown fingers traveled over the rounding of the woman's shoulder. The blanket had revealed that fair part of her anatomy, and the brave caught his breath as he imagined her naked beneath its covering.

The she spoke to him in her tongue, a speech far less harsh and guttural than his, but Grey Thunder understood none of what she said. Nor did she, his recent captive, understand any but the most basic words and phrases of the Cheyenne language. But there were other ways of communicating.

She looked up at the brave, her eyes traveling over his body, the light of desire unmistakable in those prairie flower-blue orbs. Her lips were moist, and they gleamed with the reflected light of the dying fire. And then the fair young woman spoke again, as she let the Indian blanket fall from her shoulders. She spoke in a low voice whose tone made her meaning clear, despite the fact that the man spoke little English and she even less Cheyenne.

"I hear you, Golden Woman," whispered Grey Thunder as he knelt down beside her. She had thrown off the blanket, and as he came down on his knees beside the seated woman, the brave's eyes traveled from the tips of her toes upward over the gorgeous landscape of her fair and lissome young body.

"If you were a woman of my people, I would have had to bring many horses and many presents to the teepee of your father," Grey Thunder murmured as he stroked the young blonde's high, firm breast, whose coral-pink nipple reminded him of the first flush of dawn on the plains at the beginning of spring. "But a woman such as you has never been seen in the tents of the Southern Cheyenne." The brave shook his head. "No, I am the first to take such a woman." His hand cupped her breast, and the woman gasped audibly as he gave it a gentle squeeze. "Some say you will be bad medicine," he went on, as the woman closed her eyes and pressed his hand to her bosom. "But I think you will be good medicine. I think you have been sent by the Great Spirit Who is Everywhere. I believe that your coming is a sign to my people." He smiled softly at her. "But exactly what that sign is, I do not know. I must seek out the medicine man, Walking Bear, and perhaps he will know. We shall see."

Having said this, Grey Thunder undid his breechclout and knelt naked beside his golden woman. He took her in his arms and drew her close to his body, breathing through his nostrils in great draughts as he felt the thrusting tips of her erect nipples come in contact with his chest. He heard the woman moan and press her flesh against his, and the hunger in her voice made the Cheyenne's strong heart beat faster.

"Now you are my woman," he grunted as they went down upon the buffalo robe. "I have taken you from the white men, and I shall keep you."

He was upon her now, on his hands and knees above her pale body, staring down in triumph and desire. Slowly, ever so slowly, his glance traveled down from her cornsilk hair, over her full, pouting lips and fine features, down the line of her jaw, over her swan's neck and into the softly shadowed cleft between her breasts.

"Beautiful," he rumbled, his eyes narrowing as he stared at the white woman's loveliness. "Golden Woman is beautiful. None of the daughters of the Cheyenne are like her. No other woman is her equal." He looked down again: past her delicately etched ribcage and over the gentle swell of her belly; past the curly golden fleece below, and the tumid pouting lips of her sex; and then over her trim thighs and well-turned calves, until his eye came to rest at the tips of her toes.

"Come to me," the woman murmured, her blue eyes

hidden in the shadows as they sought out Grey Thunder's dark and glittering ones.

The Cheyenne inclined his head and leaned in toward the woman, until his lips pressed the fair and smooth flesh just above the cleft between her breasts. And then the young blonde sighed as his tongue snaked its way down that soft and shadowy cleft.

Gasping as she closed her eyes, the woman shivered. Her body tensed for a moment, and then began to relax as the brave's flicking tongue skimmed over her flesh, raising goose bumps as it went, down over her belly and beyond, through the golden curls on her mound and the cleft below made by the junction of her swollen nether lips. Her thighs parted as Grey Thunder lowered his head, and the nipples of her breasts stood hard and erect.

His head bobbing gently now, the Cheyenne continued to apply his tongue to the white woman's private parts. And she, in turn, responded with sighs and heavy breathing, softly stroking the sides of Grey Thunder's face or lightly raking his gleaming black hair with her fingernails.

"Oooh, oooh," moaned the lissome young blonde, her pelvis involuntarily arching toward the ardent Cheyenne warrior's darting, stroking tongue. And as he intensified his ministrations, her passion grew and she began to murmur incoherently as the warmth and fullness of her approaching orgasm built within her with all the power of a river at floodtide.

Down and over the swollen lips of her sex and into the shadowy cleft between them went the long tongue of the Indian, gliding over the slick pink insides of those throbbing and tumid lips, flicking lightly and swiftly over the nub of the young blonde's engorged clitoris. And soon, as the first spasms of release shook the woman's body, she cried out into the shadows of the teepee.

Her eyes were closed and her hands were holding the Cheyenne's head. But it was not his name that the young blonde cried out into the shadows. It was the name of her lost lover, Dave Watson . . . the Kansan.

1

THUNDER OVER THE PLAINS

It was a time of unrest, a time of turbulence, and the Great Plains shook with thunder, with many thunders, as the fall of 1870 came. There was the great, rolling thunder of the last of the buffalo herds, as the shaggy behemoths coursed across the open prairie in the course of their migrations. There was the thunder of the storm, as the dark and swollen sky crowded the earth, sending down rain in sheets, its insistent and mounting drumming accompanied by the banshee howl of the buffeting wind. And there was one more thunder: the thunder of horses' hooves beating on the soil of the plains, as the Indians native to that area went on the warpath, and as the scouts and soldiers of the white invaders rode out to do battle with them. The plains shook to the fury of all these unleashed forces as autumn swept across the land, and no man knew where any of the rising storms of the day would break.

The young men of a number of the Plains Indian tribes had risen up against the further violations of their treaties with the United States government, and the attendant encroachment upon their lands, since the signing of the Medicine Lodge Treaty in 1868. Game grew scarce in the newly designated Indian Territory, and so the angry braves of the Cheyenne, Arapaho and Sioux nations rode north into the plains of Kansas and Colorado, back to the lands which had recently been their ancestral hunting grounds. The coming of the railroads, those steel-clad harbingers of the white man's commercial incursions, and the slaughter of the buffalo, that venerated animal which had been sent to supply man with all that he needed to live on this earth, or so the Indians of the Great Plains believed were the two geat events that colored the beginning of the eighth decade of the nineteenth century on the American frontier. And it was into this storm center that the Kansan had come, seeking vengeance and the woman he loved.

Dave Watson was out for blood. He had crossed the North American continent from east to west, and then back again; and when he had returned at last to his home state, after an odyssey which had lasted for more than two years, Dave Watson found that his sweetheart had been stolen from him. So he rode out once more, after John Hartung, the man who had taken Deanna MacPartland away from the East Kansas town of Hawkins Fork, where she had pledged to wait for him.

Accompanied by the irrepressible and resourceful newspaperman, Marcus P. Haverstraw, Dave Watson tracked John Hartung to the wild and woolly fontier town of Hays City, where the latter had recently concluded a deal with a powerful and dangerous man, one Duncan Stearns. The deal brought Hartung ten thousand dollars, as he sold Deanna MacPartland to Stearns, who was a co-owner of the Golden Slipper, the biggest saloon and sporting house in wide-open Hays City.

Deanna went quietly, fully believing that she would never see the Kansan again. She was indebted to John Hartung, who had saved her life several years earlier, when Deanna's folks were killed by rampaging Indians. She had no love for Hartung, but she did feel obliged to the man; he had also spared Dave Watson's life a few weeks earlier, leaving him incapacitated after a coach crash. Deanna had resolved to escape from Duncan Stearns once John Hartung had received payment in full; that much the blue-eyed little blonde owed the man, according to her thinking. But after that they would be quits. And then she would be free to escape from Duncan Stearns, to whose ranch John Hartung had taken her as he fulfilled the conditions of the sale and awaited the coming of the man who was about to pay him ten thousand dollars in cold cash for the Kansan's lover. And there was another man on his way to the Stearns ranch outside of Hays City, another visitor, but one whose presence was unknown to Deanna MacPartland or John Hartung. The Kansan was on the trail, and he had sworn not to rest until he had put John Hartung six feet under the ground.

Dave Watson and Marcus had come to Hays city, that wild frontier town whose marshal conducted a body count every morning after breakfast; they had come to the Kansas Pacific Railroad, whose tracks now spanned the Sunflower State. Their train journey was relatively uneventful, until the two companions were witness to one of the horrible spectacles of the time: the wanton slaughter of the buffalo herds.

In this case, Dave and Marcus saw the slaughter

from the very windows of their railroad car as the train encountered a milling, slow-moving herd of buffalo crossing the Kansas Pacific tracks. And what they saw was a frightful carnage, as "dudes and tenderfeet" (so called by the Kansan) shot at the animals from the train, killing few, but wounding and maiming many.

The wounded animals could be heard lowing pitfully as they lurched off to die in the nearby ravines. Those that were incapable of locomotion were not so fortunate, and had no alternative but to die slowly on the open prairie, tortured by their wounds as they lay beneath the glaring and pitiless sun.

Sickened by this, Dave Watson whipped out his Walker Colt and did a little shooting of his own. But it was not at the milling, defenseless buffalo, but rather at his fellow passengers. And after a time, due to a bit of fancy shooting, and a well-placed threat to the train's conductor, the Kansan had achieved his aim; soon the shooting came to a halt, and the bloodthirsty pencil-pushers, drummers, and travelers from the East put away their guns, once word spread that the Kansan was about to declare open season on any and all buffalo hunters among them. Dave Watson was smiling with grim satisfaction as he returned to his seat and shared a bottle of Old Overholt with Marcus Haverstraw.

Once they had arrived in Hays City, the two companions took up residence in an out-of-the-way hotel, intending to find John Hartung, and call the man's hand in their own good time, and on their own terms. It was then that the Kansan and Marcus Haverstraw met the lean young man in buckskins, the frontiersman with the long Indian scout's hair and small goatee, who had been a former buffalo hunter for the Kansas Pacific, and who went by the name that the railroad crews had given him, Buffalo Bill.

This man, William Frederick Cody, had saved the two companions from a serious beating during a brawl in which the Kansan and Marcus had taken on at least a dozen muleskinners. At the penultimate moment, that frozen and awful instant before Bill Cody's intervention, it looked as if Dave Watson and his newspaperman friend might well have been beaten to death. But a brace of pistol shots rang out in the heart of the Last Chance Saloon, and William F. Cody stepped in, telling the muleskinners that it wasn't a fair fight. And when those enraged men protested loudly, telling the young frontiersman to mind his own business, Cody offered to go outside and shoot it out with anyone who did not heed his orders. He was known in Hays City, and it was a tribute to his reputation that the twelve angry muleskinners suddenly lost their taste for combat and grumblingly made their way back to the bar.

Battered and bruised, Dave Watson and Marcus picked themselves up and joined Bill Cody at a table, where he had ordered a bottle of rye whiskey, and was in the process of pouring a round of drinks for his newfound friends. The men talked and drank at length, discussing the situation in Hays City, the Indian uprising on the plains, and the buffalo hunting exploits of young Bill Cody.

This last topic became an incendiary item as the drinking intensified, for it provoked strong feelings in both the Kansan and Buffalo Bill. Dave Watson, through his intimate asociation with the Pawnee tribe by way of his blood-brother, Soaring Hawk, was incensed and disgusted by the wanton and wholesale slaughter of the buffalo herds on the Great Plains. Cody, on the other hand, had been a hunter of those same animals for the Kansas Pacific Railroad.

The two men grew angrier and angrier once the Kansan had attacked Bill Cody, attaching to the young frontiersman all his negative feelings about this burning question. Cody was hurt and defensive, claiming that he only killed so that the railroad men might eat, thereby working as a force for progress and civilization. The wastefulness in butchering the dead buffalo was out of control, he maintained, wishing not to be associated with the more destructive skin hunters or the dudes and tenderfeet who shot at the herds from train windows.

A showdown was narrowly avoided, much to the relief of Marcus P. Haverstraw. The Kansan granted Bill Cody his point, telling the young man in buckskins that he had been hasty in his judgment. Buffalo Bill, in turn, was greatly taken with the way that Dave Watson had stuck to his guns in the confrontation. And the upshot of it all was that Cody had decided to aid Dave and Marcus in the search for Deanna MacPartland and John Hartung.

The next day, Cody returned to the Last Chance Saloon and reported that John Hartung had indeed been seen in Hays City, at a place known as the Golden Slipper Saloon. The biggest honkytonk and sporting house in the wide-open frontier town, the Golden Slipper was owned by two Scotsmen. The first of them was a scrawny miser named Bert Freckleton, a long-time business associate of John Hartung and the owner of a string of bawdy houses. But this was not the man to be fascinated by the beautiful Deanna MacPartland.

The man the Kansan sought was Freckleton's partner, a big, brawny redhead who had come to America from the Scottish highlands as a boy, a powerful and ruthless man named Duncan Stearns. This man, who was as daring as he was formidable, had become enamored of Deanna MacPartland, and had offered to buy her from Hartung for the enormous sum—on the frontier—of ten thousand dollars. Hartung would deliver the goods and be on his way after collecting his fee, and Deanna would be maintained as the lady of the house at Stearn's big ranch, which was located ten miles north of Hays City. But at the same time that John Hartung was making his deal with Stearns, the Kansan and his friends were closing in on him.

It was the Kansan's hope to avoid a confrontation with Duncan Stearns; he was willing to repay the man in gold, with the nuggets he had brought back from his adventures in the Idaho Territory's Boise Basin. But Stearns was a hard man, Bill Cody told the Kansan, a man who was known to come out fighting, a man who never backed down from anything . . . a man who had many guns behind him. And if they were going to face the fellow at the Golden Slipper, the frontiersman with the long, mahogany brown hair went on, they would need someone to back them up.

It just so happened that an old companion and fellow scout had ridden into town that day, and Cody immediately enlisted the man's aid. The stranger, a lanky man with long blond hair and shy, quiet ways, took to Dave and Marcus and decided to throw in with them, having no love for Duncan Stearns himself. His name, the Kansan discovered, was James Butler Hickok. His friends called him Bill. And the folks who had heard of his exploits as an Indian scout and a gunfighter called him "Wild Bill." It was with this rough and ready pair of frontiersmen, Buffalo Bill Cody and Wild Bill Hickok, that the Kansan and Marcus Haverstraw went out to their showdown with Duncan Stearns at the Golden Slipper.

Stearns had been warned, and the saloon was filled with his hired guns. Cody and Hickok remained on the main floor of the place, one armed with his Springfield buffalo gun and the other with a shotgun, while Dave Watson and the newspaperman made their way upstairs to the office of the co-owner of the Golden Slipper.

While Marcus stood guard outside the door, the Kansan confronted the big redhead in his own office. Stearns was not a man to mince words, and he told Dave Watson to ride out of Hays City and head back where he came from . . . while he was still able.

The Kansan then offered him the gold, but Stearns blew the smoke from his cheroot in Dave's face and scornfully told him to get his tail out of the Golden Slipper—pronto! "I'll not tell you again," he warned.

"You big, arrogant sum'bitch," the Kansan shot back. "I didn't come her to ask ya fer Deanna . . . I come to take her from ya." He took a step toward Duncan Stearns, clutching his fist as he did. But what the Kansan had not reckoned with was the big redhead's next move.

A tremendous brawl ensued. First, Stearns kicked off from his desk and threw himself at the Kansan, sending him flying down to the carpet on the landing outside and knocking the wind out of him. No sooner had the Kansan hit the floor than Duncan Stearns was upon him, snarling like an enraged beast as his knee caught Dave Watson foursquare in the stomach. And then the big man balled up his hamlike fist and raised it over his head, preparing to bash the Kansan's face in.

"Hey!" bellowed a startled Marcus Haverstraw, suddenly going into action as he began to recover from the shock of seeing his friend come flying through the door to Stearns' office.

Hearing this, the big redhead suddenly turned his head in the direction of the sound, an expression of surprise upon his craggy face.

Thwop! Marcus let the man have it square in the chops with a hard roundhouse right that sent him toppling off the Kansan, to roll onto the carpeted floor of the landing that overlooked the main floor of the Golden Slipper.

"Oh-h-hhh, shit!" moaned the reporter, his face a mask of pain. *"I think I broke my hand!"*

It had been a hard blow, and even a man as big and tough as Duncan Stearns had felt its force. Grunting and drooling, bleeding from both nostrils and one corner of his mouth, the big redhead writhed on the floor, shaking his head as he struggled to clear it.

This gave the Kansan the time he needed, and when the co-owner of the Golden Slipper rose unsteadily to his feet, Dave Watson was ready for him. Then, having ducked a vicious, but clumsy, overhand right, he moved in on him. *A right to the gut. A smashing uppercut to the face.* The force of this combination sent Stearns reeling back toward the railing above the main floor of the saloon.

Dave Watson steamed in and hit the man with a hard

one-two combination to the body. And then, when Stearns came up short against the wooden railing, the Kansan let him have another pair of thudding, hammerlike blows to the body.

The railing creaked, and the crowd in the saloon below cried out loudly as Dave Watson repeatedly slammed his fists into the big Scotsman's body. All of the occupants of the Golden Slipper were on their feet now, and the crowd buzzed excitedly as the two powerful men battled on the landing, separated from disaster by only the strained and sagging railing.

At each side of the Golden Slipper, Bill Cody and Bill Hickok stood poised, weapons in hand as they scanned the crowd, waiting for the bully-boys in Duncan Stearns' employ to show themselves. But no one drew a gun yet; all was quiet for the moment, as it became clear that the issue above had not been decided.

Judas Priest, this sum'bitch can shore take a beatin'! the Kansan swore to himself as the big Scotsman hung on, his back still to the railing. The Pawnees had named Dave Watson "Hammer Hand," and his punches were never less than telling, but Duncan Stearns was amazingly strong and resilient, and the big man was able to dodge a punch to the head and counter with one of his own. The crowd yelled, and then caught its collective breath as Stearns drove his fist into the belly of the Kansan, who had been carried off-balance toward his adversary by the punch he just had missed.

Then he doubled up, grunting loudly as he felt the full impact of the powerful blow. *Thwock!* Stearns followed up immediately with a flailing, overhand left which clubbed Dave Watson to the carpet. And as soon as the Kansan had hit the floor, Duncan Stearns rolled him over with a kick to the ribs.

Marcus, who had been nursing his hand all this time, rushed in at the big Scot, launching a hard right to his jaw. But Stearns, who moved with surprising alacrity for a man his size, blocked it easily and countered with a sledgehammer right of his own—one that sent the reporter flying back out of sight, to crash into the far wall of Stearns' office, and thence to collapse onto the polished hardwood floor.

Pausing to catch his breath as he watched the dazed newspaperman go down, Duncan Stearns smiled through bloodied lips, shaking his right hand and then flexing his fingers. Then he turned back to finish off the Kansan, who was already on his feet and springing at his opponent! Both men were hard as coopers' nails, and both had made the barroom brawler's fatal mistake of underestimating an enemy. In a fight where anything goes, a man should never look away until he is absolutely certain that his adversary has been beaten to a pulp and has not the least smidgin of fight left in him. But this was, unfortunately for Duncan Stearns, not the case when a bettered and bloody Dave Watson came at him.

Stearns roared with surprise—as did the excited crowd below—and started to raise his arms in order to ward off the Kansan's attack. But he was not in time, and the smaller man rammed his head into the Scotsman's face. There was a splatting sound as the Kansan's skull made contact with his enemy's face, and the force of the lunge sent Duncan Stearns backward to the railing. But at the same time that he went flying away from his opponent, he reached out reflexively and caught hold of Dave Watson's shirt with both hands.

The result of this was that both men, each weighing over two hundred pounds, went up against the wooden railing with the force of a bull buffalo going over the side of a ravine. *CR-R-R-RACK!* Suddenly, with a loud and rending sound, the railing split in two, pitching Duncan Stearns and the Kansan down onto the floor of the saloon below.

CRASH! BLUMP! The big redhead hurtled straight down to the floor, with Dave Watson's full weight upon him. He hit square in the middle of a round wooden table, collapsing its four legs with the impact of his and the Kansan's bodies. The crowd cried out in hoarse, excited voices as he hit, and somewhere at the other end of the Golden Slipper a woman screamed. The Kansan rolled off Duncan Stearns upon impact, and was on his feet no more than an instant after that, his jaw thrust foward defiantly and his big fist cocked behind his head. But Duncan Stearns had fared less well than the Kansan, and he lay still and unmoving on the floor of the saloon, eyes shut and mouth agape, with twin rivulets of blood streaming down out of his nostrils.

Stearns made no move to rise, and that was the signal for the ruffians in his employee to go into action. All hell broke loose, as Bill Cody and Bill Hickok fired their big guns at the desperadoes. By the time it was all over, six men lay dead in the sawdust of the Golden Slipper Saloon, the last of them downed by the Kansan, who had shot the man with his Derringer.

"All right, ever'body," Bill Cody called out as Bill Hickok looked around the room, smoking pistol in hand, his eyes darting with salamandrine activity. "Le's just simmer down. Don't nobody go fer his shootin' iron . . . less'n he wants to catch a dose of lead poisonin' real bad."

He scanned the room with sharp, Indian scout's eyes. "An' if I don't git to plug anybody who goes fer a gun," he paused and nodded across the room at Wild Bill, "why then, my ol' pal, Mister Hickok there will sure enough oblige with a well-placed bullet. You can bet yer granny's false teeth on that." He grinned at Hickok. "So just go easy-like, whilst me'n my friends takes care of the business we come here for in the first place."

"Sit back down, gents," ordered Wild Bill Hickok in that soft voice of his, which could now be heard clearly throughout the length and breadth of the Golden Slipper. "An' them what was standin', do it against the wall, an' by the bar—with yer hands in plain sight at all times." For an instant he was silent, scanning the room with his watery eyes. And then, when he had assured himself that all was in order, he spoke again. "Barkeep," he said, "bring me an' Mister Cody a couple of shots of rye whiskey, if ya please."

As the drinks were passed around, Bill Cody pointed out an office next to that of Duncan Stearns, telling Dave Watson that Bert Freckleton, the co-owner of the Golden Slipper, was hiding there. Hearing this, the Kansan knocked back a fast shot of rye, mounted the stairs again, and came to the locked door of the office in question, which he proceeded to kick in.

"Git up, Mister," the Kansan told the weasely-looking man who cowered behind a desk, slapping the big Walker Colt's holster as he strode into the room. "Duncan Stearns ain't in no position to tell me, so I'm askin' you: Where's Deanna MacPartland bein' kept?"

"I'll tell ye, sir-r-rrr," Bert Freckleton quavered in his

Scots burr. "But ye must fir-rrrrst pr-r-romise that ye'll no' shoot me, or an'athin' like that."

"If ya want to stay alive right now, start talkin'," the Kansan warned, his hand going down to the Colt.

"Aye, aye," the scrawny little man yelped, "I'll tell ye. Do no' shoot, fer I've nair touched so much as a hair on the wee lassie's head. Ah swear tae Gawd, mon."

"Git to the point, dammit!" the Kansan growled menacingly.

A moment later, Dave Watson came out of the office. Marcus Harverstraw was sitting on the stairs, holding a hand to his swollen and discolored jaw. The reporter looked up at his friend.

"C'mon," the Kansan told him. "We gon' take us a li'l ride. Out to Duncan Stearns' ranch...."

When Dave Watson, accompanied by Marcus Haverstraw, Buffalo Bill Cody, and Wild Bill Hickok, arrived at the Stearns ranch, the autumn moon hung low overhead. The night was crisp and clear, and even at first sight the riders could tell that the place had been attacked and put to the torch.

That was evident at a distance, and when the Kansan and his party rode closer, they could see the grisly details. Bodies littered the ground—the carcasses of horses and cattle, and the twisted forms of men, both whites and Plains Indians. The main ranch house had been burnt to the ground, its guttering embers glowing eerily in the West Kansas darkness. Several of the bunkhouses had been gutted as well, and fence of the empty corral had been torn down in one place. The riders could hear the occasional moans of the wounded, the weary, tortured lowing of maimed and dying cattle, and the high-pitched, desperate neighing of disabled horses. The sharp, acrid smell of burned wood filled the air, and the crackling of burning fence posts punctuated the sounds of the wounded and dying.

They dismounted and scoured the ruins, searching for the body of Deanna MacPartland. But there were no signs of any female presence in the charred remains of the Stearns ranch, and the Kansan silently thanked Almighty God for His mercy. But he did come upon something he recognized.

"What's that?" asked Marcus Haverstraw, as he, Bill Cody, and Bill Hickok came up behind Dave Watson.

"Looks like a man's body to me," observed young Buffalo Bill.

"Yep." agreed Hickok. "Injuns got to him."

The Kansan nodded, never taking his eyes from the bloody sight before him. "Know who that is, Marcus?" he asked the newspaperman in a hoarse whisper.

Marcus Haverstraw peered down at the bloody bundle of flesh, bone and ragged, seared clothing until he gagged and was forced to turn away. Then, after taking several deep gulps of air, the reporter said in a choked voice, "Who is it, Dave?"

"John Hartung," the Kansan said quietly causing Marcus Haverstraw to gasp at the name of Deanna MacPartland's abductor. "Took me a while to recognize him without his scalp."

"You know what happened to Deanna, Dave?" Bill Cody asked rhetorically.

"What happened to 'er, Bill?" the Kansan asked in turn, his eyes searching the frontiersman's face, as his gaze turned at last from the mortal remains of John Hartung.

"Looks like the Cheyenne got 'er," Bill Cody told him simply.

"That means she'll stay alive," Dave said hopefully.

Cody nodded.

The Kansan was quiet for a long spell. All that could be heard under the full, autumn moon was the crackling of burning and the occasional whinny of a dying horse.

"I got to git 'er back, boys," he told his friends at last.

"Well, count me in," whispered a weary-sounding Marcus P. Haverstraw.

"Bill, I reckon we can't let 'im go out there on his lonesome," Wild Bill Hickok said to his young friend.

"No sir," replied Buffalo Bill Cody, turning to Dave Watson as he did. "First we got to mosey back into Hays City an' rustle up some provisions. 'Cause we might have to be out on the plains a spell."

Then they split up to tend to the wounded, and to dispatch the maimed and suffering animals. As Dave Watson went about these grim tasks, he smiled a bitter smile as the words of a song suddenly ran through his head:

"I'm ridin' out on the windswept plain,
Where only the buffalo goes,
And men will never see me again,
Till I find my prairie rose."

2

THE BUFFALO SOLDIERS

Dust and rain, wind and grit; the howling winds that heralded winter on the open, lonely expanses of the Great Plains: this was what that Kansan faced day after day, in the autumn of 1870, as he rode over the plains and prairies of Kansas, Colorado and Nebraska in search of Deanna MacPartland, the woman he loved.

The wind keened like an Indian death song as it swept over the rolling land, rushing down from the north; and slowly, as the chill of winter's outriders began to be felt across the land, the vibrant blue sky above was bleached of all its warmth and color. The life of the plains was in retreat before the bitter winds that cut to the bone like the scalping knife of a Cheyenne warrior, retreating to burrows and lairs, to bluffs and forests. From north to south along the great central zone of the plains, men and animals alike were beginning to take refuge, the buffalo migrating and the Indians who hunted them retiring to the refuge of their winter camps, where they would huddle together by the fires in their teepees and wrapped in shaggy buffalo robes, dreaming of the spring . . . of the hunt and the glories of war.

Despite the fact that the Indian Wars were presently raging over thousands of miles of open country, as the United States Army pursued the rising tribes in the hit-and-run warfare of the frontier, almost all activity would cease with the coming of the first snows. The Indians would retire to their hidden camps; and their adversaries, the blue-coats, would retire to the safety of their stockaded forts. General Winter, who respected neither side, would sweep down and take the plains by storm, driving both whites and Indians from the field, unchallenged and irresistible until the warm, green spring offensive got under way.

Time was running out for the Kansan. He had only a few more days to locate the Cheyenne band who had taken his woman. And if he did not locate it by then, Dave Watson would be forced to sit out the winter, steeped in the bitter knowledge that he would be powerless to assist Deanna Macpartland until the coming of spring. Winter was almost upon the land; and when it came, the Kansan would lose his two invaluable friends and allies, the frontiersmen and Indian fighters Buffalo Bill Cody and Wild Bill Hickok.

Those two men, along with the dogged newspaper reporter Marcus Haverstraw, had ridden by the Kansan's side, covering long, dusty miles as they sought to pick up the trail of the war-party that had attacked the ranch of Duncan Stearns, taking Deanna MacPartland and the scalp of her erstwhile abductor, John Hartung.

As horrible as the sight of Hartung's bloody and mutilated body had been, Dave Watson viewed it with a certain grim satisfaction. The man had been a low-down sidewinder, and had done the Kansan wrong

31

more than once, causing him to promise to even the score by putting a bullet between Hartung's eyes. But the brave who killed John Hartung had repaid the debt, freeing Dave from that hard oath. He was actually relieved to learn that someone had put paid to the scoundrel's long overdue account.

What chagrined the Kansan, however, was the knowledge that he was no closer to rescuing his beloved than he and his trailmates had been at the outset of their long journey across the plains. If anything, he realized with a pang of grief, he was even farther away from his objective . . . and less able to do anything about it. The war-party had not stayed long at any one site, nor returned to any major camp, thereby complicating the pursuit immeasurably.

What Dave had learned, thanks to the trail-savvy of the two Bills, was that the band that had taken Deanna was not part of a regular Cheyenne tribal unit. Cody and Hickok, in full agreement, had identified the Indians present in the war-party by the feathering of the arrows that remained at the site of the battle. A fair number of the arrows indicated the presence of other Indians than the Cheyennes, for both Sioux and Arapaho markings had been found. This led the frontiersmen to deduce that this was an unusual band of Indians. The presence of the other arrows would have been normal in a large-scale attack, where the allied tribes had joined to present a united front in war. But a group of twenty or so, the two men reckoned, was more likely to be an outlaw conglomeration than an inter-tribal force.

Since by the evidence few Arapahoes were present, and the Sioux were a people accustomed to range the more northerly areas of the Great Plains, the Kansan's Indian-wise friends deduced that the band was led by, and composed largely of, Southern Cheyenne. "The Striped Arrow People" was one of the names that other Indians had given the formidable and extremely disciplined Cheyenne; and the name of their allies in this case was the Lakota Sioux, which name meant simply, "The Men." Along with these two came the Arapahoes, the fast friends and staunch allies of the Cheyenne, who were themselves composed of two main tribal divisions, the northern and the southern.

Never known for the strength of their numbers, the Cheyenne had done very well on the plains, due to their outstanding military abilities and the shrewdness and effectiveness of their alliances. They exalted the warrior above all things, and maintained this Spartan condition by disciplining themselves severely in the areas of sex and luxury. The chastity of Cheyenne women was a byword among the tribes of the plains, and the whites themselves had been much impressed by it. The individual Cheyenne never acquired much personal wealth, for those who were more fortunate shared with the needy among their kind, according to ancient tribal custom.

Cheyenne society was that rare and most remarkable thing, a true democracy. . . . for the men, at any rate. Virtually all the manual labor, from setting up the poles for the lodges and teepees to tanning hides, was performed by the Cheyenne females; the males attended to the tasks of hunting and rode off to war, considering physical labor outside of these pursuits to be woman's work. The tribe was composed of a number of bands which ordinarily went their own separate ways, owing to the difficulty of a life which was centered around the search for food. All of the bands met as a tribe only on such special occasions as the great rituals of the Sacred Arrow Renewal and the Sun Dance, or the joyous festival of the *Massaum,* or Animal Dance.

Another reason for coming together was the preparation for war. While the Cheyennes were governed by peace-chiefs most of the time, war-chiefs were designated to lead the braves into battle. Individual bands of Plains Indians clashed frequently, for they considered warfare a noble and necessary part of a man's life; and on occasion whole tribes warred against each other. And now, more and more, the invasions of the white men were causing the plains tribes to assemble in the face of a grave threat to the very fabric of their tribal existence.

The whites were banding the plains and prairies with steel poles and traversing them with iron horses that breathed fire, arriving in ever-greater numbers and evincing proportionately less concern for the resident Indians as their own strength grew. And they had undertaken what appeared to be the wholesale slaughter of the buffalo, the sacred animal and virtual staff of life of the Plains Indian. The fate of the buffalo and the fate of the Indian were linked, and so it was only natural for the tribes to regard this threat to their sacred beast as a direct threat to themselves.

In addition to this, the situation was further aggravated by a number of other factors. There were the white man's almost utter disregard for the treaties which had been made between the individual tribes and the Great Father in the East, and the widespread corruption and callousness of Indian agents; the ruthless profiteering of Eastern industrialists as well as frontier merchants; and the contemptuous disregard evinced by the white settlers and ranchers who had claimed portions of the Plains Indian's ancestral lands as their own. An impartial observer, although few of that stripe were to be found west of the Mississippi in the early 1870's, would have said that the tribes of the Great Plains, denied justice or legal recourse, had been pushed to the limits of their very considerable patience and tolerance, and had more than sufficient cause to go on the warpath.

The Kansan knew this. His blood-brother, Soaring Hawk, was a Pawnee. The Pawnee were the hereditary enemies of the Cheyenne, as were the Crow and the Comanches; but all were outraged at the white man's ruthless violation and exploitation of the Indian's great and ancient hunting grounds. And where the Indians had formerly befriended the few whites who had traversed the plains, they now met in mortal combat with their successors, the battlefield upon which they fought being that same, enormous expanse that constituted the heart of the American West.

"Don't look to me like we're gon' catch wind of them Injuns this side of winter," Bill Cody told the Kansan, his voice counterpointed by the creak of leather as he leaned over the side of his saddle.

"You don't think we'll catch up with 'em before then, hah?" Dave Watson asked Buffalo Bill, looking away, his heart aching as he realized that the youthful scout, Pony Express rider and buffalo hunter knew what he was talking about.

"You're gon' have to put up somewheres soon an' dig in," came a voice from his other side, the calm, drawling voice of Wild Bill Hickok.

"Yep, I reckon you boys is right," the Kansan sighed, shaking his head and forcing a tight smile as a feeling of bitter hopelessness began to rise in the pit of his stomach.

"I got to heigh me home to Louisa an' my little girl, Arta," sighed Bill Cody, looking more unhappy than Dave Watson had ever seen him in the three months they had spent together on the trail. "We got a little 'un comin' soon."

"An' I got to make me some damn money, so's I can recoup my losses at the faro an' poker tables," said Wild Bill Hickok, as the party's horses climbed a rise.

"And that means I could finally get to telegraph my Hays City story to the *Picayune*." said Marcus Haverstraw, who had written a journalistic article about the hell-raising West Kansas frontier town for the New Orleans paper which currently employed him.

"What you gon' do, Dave?" asked Bill Cody when the horses had topped the rise.

"Dunno yet," was the Kansan's terse reply, as he and the others reined in their mounts and looked across the broad expanse of gently rolling land that lay before them. Off in the distance, to the northwest, lay Fort Kingston, small as a child's log cabin, commanding a position on the high ground. "Guess I'll make up my mind when we put in at that there fort," Dave went on. "All's I want right now is to git me a hot bath, a big steak, an' a warm bed. I done had enough of the trail fer now."

"Amen to that," Marcus whispered fervently behind him.

"They say a man only needs three things in order to

be happy," Bill Hickok said quietly. "Loose boots, a tight pussy, an' a warm place to shit."

Bill Cody laughed and slapped his thigh. "I hope yer happy with them boots, Bill, 'cause the second item you mentioned is always in short supply on frontier posts. An' I ain't heard of an Army outhouse that ain't draftier than the insides of a pipe organ.

"Mebbe so," was Hickok's drawled reply. "But you can bet your buckskins the post sutler's gon' be sellin' whiskey." He licked his lips. "I'm plumb eager to wash down all this trail dust what's been cloggin' up my pipes."

"Ah yes," agreed Marcus. "I myself would not be averse to wetting my whistle, gentlemen. Not in the least."

"Well, boys," the Kansan told his saddle mates. "Le's git on down there an' enjoy the comforts of ci-vi-li-zation."

On another part of the plains, where the Republican River flows into Nebraska, less than fifty miles south of the Platte, a band of horsemen thundered over the rich soil of the riverbanks, riding away from the knifing winds that blew down from the north. The riders were on a man-hunt, and had scoured the southern plains for some time, with an intensity and singularity of purpose equal to those displayed by Dave Watson and his three companions. The two groups rode with similar motivation, but although they were all white men, they were distinguished by one great difference: the riders of the second, and larger, group were not after Indians; their quarry, it so happened, was none other than the Kansan himself.

The horsemen were twelve in number, and their leader was Duncan Stearns, the huge, fierce Scotsman who had purchased Deanna MacPartland from the late John Hartung. Stearns had survived the shoot-out at his own saloon, The Golden Slipper, and had sworn vengeance upon the Kansan and all who rode with him. And now, at the head of eleven *pistoleros,* men selected from among the roughs, desperadoes and hard cases who abounded in Hays City, the Scotsman sought the blood of the man who had dared to humiliate him in public.

There was no turning back for Duncan Stearns; he was a man who always got what he wanted and what he wanted now was Dave Watson's hide. The supreme irony of the entire business was that the Kansan, himself totally immersed in his desperate and single-minded search for Deanna MacPartland and her abductors, had no knowledge whatsoever of the big redhead's potentially lethal pursuit.

"Mister Stearns," the man on the Scotman's right said respectfully, touching his fingers to the brim of his hat as he rode up beside the co-owner of the Golden Slipper, "that there wind's gon' be a whippin' ever'thin' from its path right soon. I'd say we'd best be makin' tracks back to Hays City any day now, sir."

Duncan Stearns turned in the saddle and regarded the rider through icy blue eyes. The man's name was Tolliver. He was a halfbreed; his father had been a white man, and his mother a Crow squaw. He was a tracker and an Indian scout of considerable renown, and the Scotsman always made it a point to listen very carefully whenever the lean, walnut-brown little man addressed him.

"What do you suggest we do then, Tolliver?" he asked, nervously loosening his Colt Forty-five in its hand-tooled Mexican leather holster.

"I reckon we ought to start thinkin' 'bout gittin' ready to skeedaddle south afore the bad weather sets in," the halfbreed replied. "Ain't nobody goin' nowheres on the plains fer the next three-four months, Mister Stearns. After that, why, we can try to pick up that fella's trail once't things warms up."

"Well, Custer played hell with the Cheyenne on the Washita in the dead of winter," Stearns reminded Tolliver.

The scout turned away and sent a brown gob of tobacco juice splattering against the hard prairie earth. Then, wiping his mouth with the back of his leather-gloved hand, he turned back to face the big redhead.

"You got to recollect there was one helluva lot of troopers with Colonel Custer back in '68, Mister Stearns," the halfbreed reminded him. "An' them blueboys was all supplied fer their long winter's march." Here Tolliver chuckled and shook his head. "Nonetheless, ol' Hard Ass Custer done run them boys of his into the ground. He never was much fer lookin' after his troops, y'know." He grinned wryly at Duncan Stearns. "No civilian cowpokes'd ever put up with conditions bad as those was. Only the poor devils in the United States Army. They got to take it. An' besides, the Cheyenne ain't 'bout to let somethin' like that happen again."

"That's how Little Phil intends to break the back of Indian resistance," growled the Scotsman, referring to

General Sheridan, the commander of the army's Department of the Missouri, whose territory comprised the greater part of the frontier.

"Even Little Phil hisself couldn't git these here hombres to go a-gallivantin' all over the plains in the middle of winter, Mister Stearns," Tolliver quietly told his employer, jerking his head back in the direction of the *pistoleros* who rode behind them. "In my opinion, best thing you can do is put up fer the winter, an' then hightail it out again once't the spring comes."

"I suppose you're right," the big man growled, frowning as he turned in his saddle and cast a cold eye upon the horsemen behind him. All right. Back to Hays City it is." There was a steely glint in his pale blue eyes as he said this."

"But I'll be back," Duncan Stearns growled, looking out over the vast expanse of open, empty land before him. "And I'll run that Watson to the ground and settle the score with him if it's the last thing I do on earth. So help me, God!"

Fort Kingston was a sprawl of single-story, wooden frame buildings, the ground between them dotted with scrub bushes and an occasional stunted tree. The best-looking buildings, the Kansan noticed as he and his friends rode into the army post, were those in which the officers were quartered. There were a number of stable buildings in evidence, which told him that the post housed a sizeable cavalry troop in addition to its regiment of infantry. And out on the parade ground, riders wheeled their prancing steeds and passed in revue as a military band played a Civil War tune which had re-tained its popularity on the western posts of the United States Army:

"When Johnny comes marching home again, Hurrah!
  Hurrah!
We'll give him a hearty welcome then, Hurrah!
  Hurrah!
The men will cheer,
The boys will shout,
The ladies they will all turn out,
And we'll all feel gay when Johnny comes marching
  home. . . ."

"Hey look," Dave Watson cried out in amazement as he watched the distance cavalrymen handle their big horses with great style. "Them fellas is 'most all colored!"

"All but the officers," Bill Cody told him. "That's the Tenth Cavalry. There's 'bout four different outfits like theirs—cavalry an' infantry—fightin' Injuns, north an' south. The officers is all white, but the troppers is black to a man." Cody nodded. "An' let me tell you, they're a bunch of tough boys, with discipline an' morale at least the equal of any white outfit. They give the Injuns hell whenever they tangle with 'em. The Injuns call 'em the Buffalo Soldiers."

"Buffalo Soldiers?" echoed Marcus Haverstraw. "Why on earth do they call them that?"

"It's on account of the hair of the Negro soldiers," Bill Hickok told him quietly. "Reminds 'em of buffalo fur. An' I reckon that's a term of respect, 'cause the buffalo's a sacred animal fer the Injun."

"That's right interestin'," Dave Watson said as Marcus took a small notebook out of his coat pocket and began to scrawl notes in it with the stub of a pencil.

"Marcus, you gon' have one big pile of notes purty soon," Bill Cody said to the newspaperman, grinning at Wild Bill Hickok and the Kansan as he did.

"Well," grunted Marcus, as he finished writing and thrust the notebook back inside his pocket, "what goes on out here in the West is big news to the rest of the country. Your friend Ned Buntline has proven that. He's making a pretty penny on those dime novels he keeps turning out about you, Bill. And so is another scrivener, a fellow by the name of Colonel Prentiss Ingraham. He's written even more books than Buntline."

Buffalo Bill scowled at the mention of these names. "Humph!" he snorted, fretting as he slapped his buckskins, raising a cloud of trail dust. "Them fellas is makin' a fortune tellin' folks 'bout what I done, an' I ain't hardly seen a penny of that money. An' I'm the hero of them damn stories." He shook his head. "It don't seem fair. I may be livin' out here in communion with nature, an' all that but I got bills to pay, just like the next man."

"In that case, you ought to do something about it," Marcus Haverstraw told him.

Buffalo Bill pushed back the brim of his broad leather hat and scratched his forehead. "What d'ya mean?" he asked the reporter. "What-all could I do?"

"Well, if I were you, Bill," Marcus replied, staring into the eyes of the rangy, brown-haired young man, "I'd go East and get me a piece of the action"

"I been east," Cody told him. "Once't I rid all the way to Omaha."

His companions laughed at this.

Smiling as he shook his head, Marcus said, "I meant a bit farther East than that. New York City, for instance. That's where the money's to be made."

"But what would I do there?" asked a puzzled Cody.

"Why, you're already a national hero," Marcus told him. "You'd be a celebrity—wined and dined by all the best people, written about in all the newspapers."

"Don't sound like there's a helluva lot of money in any of that," Buffalo Bill told him. "An' even if there was, how would I go about gittin' my share of it?" He was watching the newspaperman with interest now.

"Well, for openers you would get on Ned Buntline and that old hack, Prentiss Ingraham, and tell them you want a share of the profits. You could possibly strike a deal with their publishers, as well. And then. . . . who knows?" There was a faraway look in the newspaperman's eyes as he leaned forward in the saddle, lost in thought for the moment.

"Why you could rustle up a bunch of cowboys and even a few tame Indians," he said in a sudden access of enthusiasm, a smile now brightening his face. "And you could take this collection of specimen from place to place—around the country, perhaps—giving your own presentation."

"What sort of presentation, ol' hoss?" the Kansan asked, his interest awakened by the journalist's scheme.

"Oh, I don't exactly know," Marcus replied, squinting as he concentrated. "A stage piece, perhaps. Or maybe some sort of outdoor spectacle. . . . some sort of representation of life on the frontier—in the 'Wild West'."

"You mean like a circus?" asked Wild Bill Hickok, his eyes narrowing as he studied Marcus Haverstraw's features.

"Ah, something like that, I expect," was the newspaperman's reply. "In essence. It would be the western equivalent of a circus."

"I don't know what to make of such a far-fetched idea," Bill Cody told Marcus Haverstraw, pulling the brim of his hat back down over his broad forehead. "I guess I'll just have to give it some thought when I'm back home with Louisa an' little Arta this winter."

At the mention of his wife, a glum expression overspread the young frontiersman's countenance. But this sudden access of melancholy was not to be of long duration.

"Hey, lookee there," a reedy voice called out as the four companions walked their horses toward the stable compound. "Ain't that Buffalo Bill?"

"Jubilation!" growled a rich bass voice. "It sure as hell is! Hey, Bill Cody, how you doin'?"

Buffalo Bill's face lit up as he heard this. He turned in the direction of the voices, grateful for having been wrenched back to the present, away from the morose thoughts of a reunion with his wife Louisa.

"Why, if it ain't the ol' Sarge!" he called out in delight, having recognized one of the black soldiers who had addressed him. "An' there's Corp'ral Homer, as well. Why, I'll be a son of a gun!" He wheeled his horse around and started over to a small cluster of black troopers who were lounging outside the entrance to the post sutler's store. And as he did, William Frederick Cody was grinning from ear to ear.

"I see you're still of a piece," remarked the man with the rich bass voice, holding out his hand as the frontiersman came near.

"Yep," Bill Cody replied, leaning over in the saddle

to take the man's hand. "I guess I been right lucky, Sarge. Why, the onliest thing I got to regret at this very moment is meetin' my little woman again."

The black troopers laughed. Cody shook the hand of the sergeant with the deep voice, and then did the same with the corporal who stood beside him.

"We been runnin' into some of yer old friends, Bill," said the corporal with the reedy voice, a tall, well-made, and handsome young fellow with a pencil moustache. "The Cheyenne is mighty riled up these days—the young bucks, that is. They's mighty sore about the Medicine Lodge Treaty."

"Yep," growled the bass-voiced sergeant, a big bear of a man with a bull neck and bright, intelligent eyes. "The Great White Father in Washington done slipped it to 'em again."

"How you boys been doin'?" Cody asked the black troopers, as his companions walked their horses over to join him.

"Been busy," the burly sergeant told him. "Cheyenne, Sioux an' Arapaho bucks is kickin' up a mighty ruckus these days. So we been out on the plains more often than not, tryin' to catch hold of 'em."

"Catchin' Injuns on the open prairie's like tryin' to pick up quicksilver with yer fingers," the corporal commented.

"You ain't lyin' there, Homer," Bill Cody agreed. Then he turned to his companions and pointed to each in turn, and calling out his name. After that he turned back to the black troopers. "Boys, them's my current trail mates. An' me an' Mister Hickok goes back a ways, as you prob'ly know. An' I want you fellas," he said looking over his shoulder at Hickok, Marcus and the Kansan, "to meet a couple of pals from my army scoutin' days: Sergeant Wardell Bumstead an' Corp'ral Homer White."

The men shook hands and greeted each other.

"We been on the lookout for Cheyenne our own selves," Buffalo Bill informed the black troopers. "Outlaw band, mostly Cheyenne, some Sioux an' Arapaho. They done stole my friend Dave's sweetheart away." He looked from the troopers to the Kansan and then back again. "Mebbe you done run across 'em. The young lady's name was—uh, *is!* Deanna MacPartland." Cody's face reddened and he glanced apologetically toward the Kansan. "You heard anything, Wardell?" he went on, turning back to the bull-necked sergeant.

Wardell Bumstead nodded his head. "That could be a young buck by the name of Grey Thunder," he told Buffalo Bill. "Some of our fellas had a brush with his band. They's a bunch of wild-ass bastards, them lads. An' our Injun scouts been sayin' as how he got hisself a white woman."

"Now that's a fact," seconded Corporal Homer White, looking up at the Kansan. "They say he calls 'er Golden Woman. An' that he done made her *his* woman."

As he heard this, Dave Watson's face grew dark as a thunder cloud, and his knuckles went white as his hands clenched his broad leather gunbelt. Cody, Hickok and Marcus had all turned in his direction, looking to see how the Kansan would react to this intelligence.

"You know where this Grey Thunder happens to be these days, Sarge?" he asked Wardell Bumstead in a low, tense voice.

The black trooper shook his head. "Our fellas had a brush with him an' his pals way back in July, Mister Watson. An' that's the last we done heard of him."

The Kansan turned to Bill Cody. " 'Sounds like the fella I'm lookin' fer."

Cody nodded. "It sure enough does."

"I'd say it was a right good bet," seconded Bill Hickok.

"I'm gon' keep after that sucker," the Kansan told his companions, a steely glint coming into his eye.

"You ain't gon' find him after the first snowfall," Buffalo Bill reminded him. "So you jus' better sit tight for the winter."

The Kansan's face was an expressionless mask as he sat in the saddle, but his inner state was one of utter agony, tormented as he was by the thought of his beloved Deanna at the mercy of the hostile known as Grey Thunder.

"Yep," he said hollowly, looking down at the ground before him. "I reckon you're right, Bill. I got to wait."

"That's the spirit, ol' hoss," Wild Bill Hickok said softly as he slapped the Kansan on the back. "She'll be all right, I reckon. Ain't nothing more gon' happen to her over the winter."

"Bill's right," seconded Buffalo Bill. "If she come this far, chances are she's bein' taken care of in the Injun camp. You jus' got to be patient, Dave."

The Kansan nodded tiredly. "I hear you right enough, Bill," he said in that hollow and tired voice. "That's what I got to do."

"C'mon, boys," said Bill Hickok. Le's stable these here horses an' then mosey over to the sutler's store so's we can git us a drink."

"We'll see you later, gents," Buffalo Bill told the black troopers as he and his companions began to walk their horses over to the stables.

"We was hopin' you been sent here to shoot some buffalo," Sergeant Wardell Bumstead called out in a wistful tone of voice.

"Y'all be doin' us a big favor if ya do, Bill," added Corporal Homer White. "That damn Army grub ain't got no better than it was last time you done et it."

" 'Fraid I got to head home an' feed my own family first," Bill Cody called back over his shoulder as his horse took him into the stable.

Once the horses had been attended to and stabled, the Kansan and his companions made their way over to the big wooden structure that served as the headquarters building for Fort Kingston. There they made their presence on the post known to a grizzled sergeant major, and then inquired as to whether the post commander possessed any knowledge of the whereabouts of Grey Thunder and his band of hostiles.

The sergeant major, whose yellow-trimmed jacket proclaimed him a cavalryman, was an old campaigner named Curtis O. McDaniel. He was delighted to make the acquaintance of such a pair of redoubtable scouts and Indian fighters as Buffalo Bill Cody and Wild Bill Hickok. The post commander, Colonel Leonidas B. Scarborough, was not on the post at present, and was not expected back for several days. His second-in-command, Major Dalton Lanier, was at the moment inspecting a stagecoach depot which the Army had decided to fortify in response to the increasing pressure of Indian attacks.

"I 'spect the major'll be back afore the sun goes down," Sergeant Major McDaniel told the four visitors. He as a squat, jowly man with iron-grey hair and a gleaming skin the color of Number Nine coal. "Whyn't you gentlemen take yerselves over to the sutler's store an' rest a spell? An' when Major Lanier comes back, I'll send an orderly to fetch you."

"Sounds like a good idea to me," mumbled Wild Bill.

"I reckon we'll jus' mosey over there, Sarn't McDaniel," Buffalo Bill told the man, smiling at the thought of a good stiff drink. "Why, I'll bet ol' Wardell Bumstead an' Homer White is jus' dyin' to spring for a few drinks in honor of our reunion."

"You know them two rascals?" McDaniel asked the young frontiersman, looking up from his paperwork, a puckish grin on his face."

"Yep," was Cody's reply. "Got to know ol' Wardell an' Homer right good a couple of years back, when I was scoutin' an' huntin' buffalo fer the Army."

"In that case," the old veteran rumbled, "I don't have to tell you not to play poker nor to roll no bones with them two troopers, now, do I? They's holy terrors when it comes to winnin' other folks' money."

"That aint my speciality, Sarge," Cody told McDaniel. "But ol' Wild Bill here don't give way to no man at the poker table."

Hickok flushed at this, looking toward the door as he shuffled his feet restlessly.

"That damn Wardell has got him the kind of mem'ry what allows him to recollect every single card was what dealt out visible-like in the hand," Sergeant Major McDaniel informed the four companions.

"Well, Sarge, I reckon that's what it's rightly all about," Wild Bill murmured shyly, his eyes now on the tips of his boots. "Good gamblin' has a hell of a lot more to do with odds an' percentages than it does with luck an' bluffin'."

"So long as you know that, I reckon you'll be all right, Bill," McDaniel told Hickok. "Jus' remember that ol' Wardell is a sly dog."

"I'll shore keep that in mind, thank ya," muttered Wild Bill, as he and his companions filed out of the headquarters building.

"You aim to do some gamblin'?" the Kansan asked Wild Bill.

"Reckon I do, Dave," the frontiersman replied. "If they's any action hereabouts."

"Oh, there'll be action, all right," Bill Cody told him, "if ol' Wardell an' Homer has set themselves down at a table."

When the companions entered the post sutler's store they were greeted by the sounds of music and men's voices; by the strong smells of tobacco smoke and rye whiskey; by the clicking of shaken dice and the riffle of shuffled playing cards. The back room of the place was a rectangular space, forty feet long by twenty feet wide, whose floor was dotted with tables and chairs. At the near end of the room men sat and read newspapers and books, played music on banjos and harmonicas, or merely sat together on old horsehair sofas, telling jokes, swapping war stories and tall tales, or just engaging in the soldier's perennial pastime of griping. The far side of the room was taken up by a number of tables where the black infantrymen and cavalrymen played cards; and in an open space by a corner a number of men knelt and threw dice, crying out loudly in counter-pointed joy and despair each time a player made his point or crapped out. It was plain to see that gambling, although illegal in principle on military establishments, flourished at Fort Kingston, as it did on many of the other western posts.

Cody and Hickok were immediately recognized by the greater number of soldiers present, and the Kansan was impressed as he began to realize just how famous his two companions really were. Bill Cody was still in his early twenties and Bill Hickok had barely turned thirty yet the yarns of their various exploits had already been woven into the fabric of legend by word of mouth (which naturally gave rise to frontier tall-tales) and the intentional exaggerations of the dime novelists back East. And this was only the beginning, Dave Watson told himself.

What would be the result if these two young men chose to actively participate in the creation of their own legends? the Kansan wondered. For by his conversations with the worldly and well-travelled Marcus P. Haverstraw, he had learned that a new element had been introduced into the traditional process whereby men became renowned for their exploits and service to their fellow-men. Commerce was the name of this new element, and it was attended by its handmaiden, Publicity.

A great and sudden change was underway in America, Marcus had told Dave. Certain individuals had mastered the dubious art, or skill, of turning the fame of popular heroes to their own profit. The dime novels, which exploited the feats of men such as Cody and Hickok, were prime examples of this new trend whereby writers made a living and publishers made a killing through the intentional exploitation, distortion and exaggeration of the deeds of popular figures. The products of this collaboration reached hitherto unthought-of thousands, and literally created a new set of popular legends. What would happen, the Kansan asked himself, if Buffalo Bill and Wild Bill were actually to immerse themselves in the golden stream of this most potent and influential process, this lurid new activity which had hitched the dynamics of American go-get-em' salesmanship to the freighted wagon of popular mythology?

Dave Watson had no idea what the future held for either man, as he accompanied them into the heart of the Fort Kingston sutler's store, but he was sure that life would rarely be dull for the two of them. Marcus Haverstraw, using his newspaperman's savvy, had told Cody to go East and make his fortune, but the buckskinned young frontiersman was not yet ready to consider such a possibility. What the shy and taciturn Wild Bill Hickok thought was anyone's guess, for he was a man who played his cards close to the vest. Suddenly, Dave was roused from his reverie as the voices of the troopers began to ring out through the sutler's store.

"Hey Bill, did ya plug any Injuns lately?"

"What'cha huntin' today, Mister Cody—buffaloes or John Barleycorn?"

"Bill Hickok—you still out trackin' Injuns fer Uncle Sam?"

"Hey, Bill, you done brung us any buffalo meat? The grub what they used to serve in the Conferderate prisoner-of-war camps was a heap better'n the slop we

gits here."

"Lookee, fellas—look at that big ol' rifle Bill Cody's a-totin'!"

"Bill Cody, how's 'bout tellin' us how ya shot that Injun dead when you was only a lad of eleven?"

"Damn," Buffalo Bill swore under his breath as he smiled a wry smile at the Kansan. "That Injun has been hitched to my name like a tin kettle to a dog's tail."

"You still ridin' scout fer Little Phil?"

"Bill Hickok, you still play poker?"

This last question was asked by a grinning Sergeant Wardell Bumstead, as the four companions approached the table at the far end of the sutler's store, where he and Corporal Homer White sat playing cards with several other black troopers.

"I shorely do, Wardell," Hickok answered quietly as one of the troopers vacated a seat and offered it to him. "An' I'm hankering to have my drinks an' dinner paid fer with money outta yer pocket."

The powerfully-built sergeant chuckled at this. "Well, you jus' sit down an' make yourself to home, an' then we'll sho' 'nuff see who pays fer what with whose money." He looked around at Dave, Marcus and Bill Cody. "We got us room at this here table fer several more." He gestured expansively. "How 'bout it, gents?"

"Don't mind if I do," said Bill Cody, pulling up a newly vacated seat.

"I'd prefer to observe, if you don't mind," Marcus Haverstraw told the black seregeant. "Suit yourself," was the reply. "An' how 'bout you?" Bumstead asked, grinning as he caught the Kansan's eye.

"Well, I ain't much at cards," Dave told him. "An'

from what I done heard, I'll be playin' way out of my depth. But I think I'll set in fer a spell, Sarge."

"That's the spirit," Homer White murmured approvingly as Wardell Bumstead shuffled and cut the cards with an impressive display of manual dexterity.

"First we want a drink," Bill Hickok said, raising his small voice as he opened his coat to reveal the gleaming pistol holstered beneath it. The holster itself was tied to his lean thigh with a thong of rawhide, after the manner of a professional gunman.

Bumstead and White noticed this immediately, and were much impressed.

"You still practice the quick-draw, Mister Hickok?" the corporal asked as his companion motioned for the sutler to bring a bottle of rye whiskey to the table.

"That I do, Corp'ral," murmured Wild Bill, shyly looking away from the table as he did.

This was something which had impressed the Kansan continually in the course of his time on the trail in the company of Hickok. Every day without fail, the man would practice his draw. Hickok had never fired his six-gun, since it was always possible that Indians were within hearing distance, but he practiced his draw with an intensity and concentration which Marcus had likened to that of a great musician. A virtuoso would bring those qualities to the daily practice of his instrument; and Wild Bill practiced his quick-draw in much the same fashion. The man was a virtuoso of the firearm, Marcus had told the Kansan, an example of the new breed of specialist which had arisen in response to the unique conditions of frontier life in the American West. Hickok was fast and accurate, an artist whose mind and body were trained to work in near-perfect harmony whenever he pursued the exercise of his lethal art.

Wild Bill was master of a rare skill, the Kansan acknowledged with a certain degree of admiration. But it was a speciality which created enemies at least as fast as it created many more potential adversaries, relatives of his victims out for revenge or young bucks out to prove themselves. Dave recalled the Greek myth in one of his uncle Ethan's books, the one where dragon's teeth were sown like seeds, and armed men sprang up from them. Wild Bill was sowing dragon's teeth.

Dave wondered what life held in store for his friends; for unlike their counterparts who had gained renown playing musical instruments, the vituosi of the six-gun were not celebrated for their longevity. And whereas one great musical artist might be superseded by his rival in popularity, there was certainly room in the profession for both of them; but in the West, the man who came in second best was buried.

Oh, Cody and Hickok would have colorful and exciting futures, Dave Watson told himself. He had absolutely no doubt about it.

The bottle of rye arrived at the table, and Bill Cody poured drinks all around.

"To the lads of the Tenth Cavalry," he called out in a ringing voice once he had finished pouring, rising from his seat as he held his shotglass in the air. "To the finest, most dogged, most ass-kickin' bunch of horse soldiers there is!"

"Hear, hear!" chorused the roomful of black troopers, each man rising to his feet and joining in the toast.

"To Buffalo Bill Cody an' Wild Bill Hickok,'" bellowed Wardell Bumstead, once a second round of drinks had been poured. "To the finest Injun scouts an' all-'round buckaroos in the whole damn West!"

"Hear, hear!" shouted the black cavalrymen, toasting the celebrated pair with overwhelming enthusiasm.

"An' now," Homer White said as he and the others took their seats once more and settled down at the table, "le's git down to business an' play us some poker."

And so they did. The Kansan found himself no match for Hickok and the two black troopers, and soon dropped out of the game. He had lost twenty dollars, and felt that was more than enough, for he was not a gambling man at heart.

Bill Cody had lost a bit more, and soon folded as well. Dave had noticed the young frontiersman grow progressively more glum over the past two days; he attributed this condition to Cody's obvious reluctance to return to his wife, Louisa.

William F. Cody was not happily married, the Kansan had learned in the course of his acquaintance with the man. While Buffalo was fast becoming a legend to most of the citizens of the Republic, he remained a constant disappointment to his proper young wife. Louisa Cody's ideal was one of stability and respectability. She wanted a man who would aspire to be one of the pillars of the community, a man on whose arm she would be proud to be seen; a man who would come home after work and read the Holy Bible to his adoring family. But this was not exactly how Bill Cody was disposed to behave. Louisa did not, apparently, ever accept the man as he was, and this naturally created a great deal of unhappiness for Buffalo Bill and his spouse, because neither one of them gave the other what he or she really wanted.

Marry in haste, repent at leisure, Dave told himself as he reached for the bottle of rye. Seated at his left was Marcus Haverstraw, who watched the poker game as he watched almost everything else—with consuming interest. The man had the gift of curiosity, and was interested in almost all things; he was especially fascinated by the endless diversity of human behavior. The Kansan grinned as he poured a hooker of rye whiskey for his friend. Boredom and Marcus P. Haverstraw, he realized with a pang of envy, were total strangers.

An hour later, an orderly entered the back of the sutler's store and made his way over to the table where Bill Hickok and the black troopers were playing poker.

"Sar'nt Bumstead," the orderly said crisply, popping his boot heels together as he came to attention before the burly non-commissioned officer. "Compliments of Sar'nt Major McDaniel. Major Lanier requests the prsence of Messers. Cody, Hickok, Watson an' Haverstraw at his dinner table. He expects 'em there in half an hour's time."

"Shit, piss an' corruption," growled Wardell Bumstead. "Ol' Bill Hickok's got him a pile of my greenbacks. Damn McDaniel's ass!"

"That come down from the top, Wardell," Homer White told him with a sigh, throwing down his cards in disgust as the orderly executed an about-face and marched off smartly. He, too, had lost a considerable sum to Wild Bill. "ain't no use in layin' it at McDaniel's feet."

"Three queens,'" Hickok said quietly, turning over his cards and laying them down.

"Bullocks," muttered Wardell Bumstead, slapping his own cards face-down upon the table. "Y'all come back soon, Bill," he said, smiling peevishly as he looked up at Hickok. "I'd like to git another crack at ya."

"I'll shore do what I can, Wardell," Wild Bill promised as he raked in the pile of greenbacks on the table-top. "Been nice playin' with you fellas," Hickok grunted. "We gon' go an' freshen us up some."

"C'mon, let's get us some grub," Bill Cody told the others as he stood up abruptly. "We been on the trail so long I plumb forgot what real food is like."

The meal, as it turned out, was an absolute delight after the rigors of the trail. Venison, sweet and white potatoes, gravy, spinach, string beans, home baked bread, and apple pie served with cordials and coffee; these constituted the rich and hearty fare at the table of Fort Kingston's acting commander.

"Gee, I don't know what-all them boys in the sutler's store was bitchin' 'bout," a wide-eyed Dave Watson whispered to Bill Hickok as the dinner was served.

"This is what the *officers* git to eat," was Wild Bill's quiet reply. "Compared to what these fellas has, the enlisted men eats like dogs. They don't git none of this here fresh meat an' vegetables. What they eat a whole lot of is stuff like mouldy meat, suspicious stews, beans, hardtack, an' salt pork. It ain't no picnic eatin' beside them poor devils, believe me."

"Sergeant Major McDaniel informs me that you gentlemen are out in search of Grey Thunder and his band of hostiles," Major Lanier said with just the slightest trace of a Southern accent, opening the conversation at the table.

"Yessir, that's a fact," Bill Cody replied, chewing on a forkful of steaming venison haunch. "But that boy don't ever settle down long enough fer a body to catch up with him."

"Well, he'll have to settle down soon enough," the major told him. "Winter's coming up mighty fast."

"Yessir, it is," agreed the buckskinned frontiersman. "An' me an' ol' Bill has got to git home fer a spell, an' take care of things. An' Miter Haverstraw here—he's a newspaper reporter, Major—is gon' file some of his western stories an' reports. He works fer the *New Orleans Picayune*. An' my friend, Dave Watson, is gon' "

"I'm gon' keep after that sum'bitch, Major," the Kansan told Lanier suddenly, interrupting Buffalo Bill. "I just now made up my mind 'bout that."

A dead silence greeted this announcement, and the Kansan took the opportunity to study each of the four faces that were now turned toward him.

Major Lanier, knowing full well the rigors of a winter campaign, frowned disapprovingly, staring hard at the audacious young man who had just decided to pursue the band of hostiles despite the counsel of more experienced hands. Marcus Haverstraw just stared open-mouthed at his old friend, stupefied by Dave Watson's words, by a declaration which the reporter considered tantamount to an announcement of impending suicide. Bill Cody and Bill Hickok, old hands on the plains and old Indian fighters, looked at the Kansan through grave eyes which reflected sorrow, compassion and resignation. They both understood his need to go, and they both understood that if he did, the odds were a hundred to one that he would never return alive.

"I want to thank you boys for all that ya done," Dave Watson said quietly, not meeting anyone's eye at this uncomfortable moment. "An' I want to thank you fer yer hospitality, Major Lanier," he went on. "Y'see, I'll be ridin' out in the mornin'. . . ."

The wind keened and moaned like a restless spirit, and the sagebrush whipped back and forth under its lavishing gusts; clouds of dust issued from gullies and ravines, and the tumbleweed flew over the hard earth in drifting, erratic courses. The sky above was the color of lead, and the few clouds to be seen were dingy, and hung ominously low. A light coating of hoarfrost gave the rocks on the ground a silvery patina, and the shrubs and prairie grass were brown and sere.

A small band of Indians huddled in their blankets as they fought their way up a steep rise, heading directly into the cold, knifing wind. The party was comprised of three men and women, and five children, whose ages ran from six months to ten years of age. They were reservation Indians, Crows who had taken to the white man's ways, peaceful farmers who tilled the soil at the nearby Blacksburg Reservation, in which direction they were presently headed.

Leading the small band was an old Indian whom the local whites called Tommy One-Eye. His real name was Black Owl. He had lost his eye decades ago, fighting the Cheyenne, in the days before he recognized the futility of resisting the advance of the white men, whose numbers were as the leaves of the trees. With him were his brother-in-law, Deer-Finder, and his son, Sharp-Axe. They were accompanied by their respective wives and children. The group had recently visited their people at a tribal conclave, and were now headed back to the reservation, which was located ten miles south of the town of Hubner's bend, on the River Platte.

The cold had come suddenly, even more quickly than the Indians had expected, and Black Owl was doing his best to reach the reservation before nightfall. Camping out in such weather was not to his liking, although the whites and Indians had long been at peace in this area. But Black Owl preferred to push for the relative comfort of his home on the Blacksbug Reservation.

Home was now less than ten miles away, the Crow realized with a feeling of satisfaction as his old and spavined horse fought its way to the top of the rise. And when he gained the highest position on the surrounding prairie, Black Owl saw a cloud of dust to the north, almost straight ahead of him, rising in streamers that were almost immediately dissipated by the swirling winds.

The dust meant that horsemen were aproaching, a fair number of them, judging by the size of the cloud. At this distance it was impossible to tell whether they were Indians or whites, but Black Owl was not particularly worried, in any case. There had been peace in the country for so long that the old Indian took it for granted that the riders were engaged in some peaceful pursuit. Their paths would cross before long, the old Indian realized, for his band was headed on a course that would bring it very close to the riders up ahead. But that was not a matter of much concern to Black Owl, for he and his people had no enemies in this part of the land.

The horsemen drew closer, and the Crow was able to

see that they were whites. This did not alarm him, because he knew that no one had recently broken the peace in this country. But his eyesight had been failing him lately, and the old man did not see that the band of horsemen was advancing upon his party with rifles and pistols drawn. And when Sharp Axe apprised him of this, Black Owl muttered to himself in his confusion.

"What is this thing? Why do these white men come armed? Someone must have done a bad thing, and this must be the war-party that the whites call a posse. This is no threat to us. Surely they must see the women and children? And we do not even have guns."

The old man turned and confided his thoughts to his followers, who were reassured by his words. And so they made ready to ride on, toward the oncoming party of armed white men. All would be well, Black Owl had told them; and no one in the little band could conceive of the riders' doing violence to such a mixed and unarmed group of peaceful Indians.

Several moments later the crack of pistols and the bark of rifles were heard above the howling wind. Black Owl cried out in surprise and waved his empty hands over his head, calling out to the oncoming riders in their own language, shouting that he was a reservation Indian, on his way home, that his family and relatives were with him. But the old man's hoarse cries were abruptly silenced as a slug from a Winchester smacked into his chest with a dry, slapping sound sending him to the hard ground, toppling him backward off his horse.

The next volley of shots caught Sharp Axe and two of the women. Deer-Finder cried out in rage and strung an arrow to his hunting bow, yelling all the time for the horsemen to hold their fire. But he was gunned down before he had a chance to launch his arrow, along with several of the children and two of the dogs that pulled the band's three travois.

"Stop! Stop, you fools!" cried Sharp Axe, blood running down the sides of his mouth as he raised himself up from the ground on quivering arms. The horsemen were almost upon the group now, and he could see the cold eyes and hard faces of the gunmen; and in that moment the dying brave knew that no mercy would be shown to any of his people who had managed to survive the first onslaught. And then he looked up into the eyes of the man whose horse pranced and snorted not ten feet in front of him. The man was trying to calm the animal down, so that he could draw a bead on him. The man was big, with bright red hair and icy blue eyes. Those killer's eyes were the last thing that Sharp Axe saw before the man shot him.

The horsemen were not finished. At the orders of the big man, they rode around the fallen and pumped lead into living and dead alike, into squalling infants and still old men. And then, when their leader was finally satisfied, the riders holstered their pistols and sheathed their rifles, sparing only an occasional and casual glance for the carnage which they had just wrought. A moment later, at a curt signal from the big, redheaded man, they rode off without a word, leaving the bodies of the slaughtered Crow Indians—man, woman and child—to stare up at the leaden sky with accusing and unseeing eyes.

Duncan Stearns was smiling as he rode off at the head of his band of desperadoes, happy to have gotten a chance to avenge himself upon the redskinned bastards who had burned his ranch to the ground and stolen Deanna MacPartland from him. And he smiled at the memory of what had transpired moments before the massacre. . . .

"But them Injuns up there couldn't've had nothin' to do with the attack on yer place, Mister Stearns," Tolliver, the half-breed scout, had protested when the riders first caught sight of the little band of Crows.

"They're Indians aren't they, goddam it!" Stearns growled, his face purpling with anger. "Do you think they have any scruples when it comes to killing white folks? Not on your life! We all look the same to them, and they couldn't give a hoot in hell who they kill—just so long as he or she is white."

"Now, I don't hold with that, Mister Stearns," Tolliver replied, sitting up straight in the saddle. "Them's just peaceable Injuns, most likely from the Blacksburg Reservation, which ain't far from here."

"You'll shut your mouth and do what you're told, by God!" the Scotsman roared, his eyes blazing with hatred as he looked down at the scout.

"It's murder, an' I ain't gon' sit here an' let you turn these hard cases loose on them poor unarmed Injuns out there. His hand went down slowly to the Smith and Wesson that was holstered by his side.

Seeing this, Duncan Stearns froze in the saddle and did not move . . . save for a slight nod of the head in the direction of a curly-headed, scar-faced man who rode a few feet behind Tolliver.

"Now, call off these boys, Mister Stearns," the scout ordered, slipping his pistol out of its holster.

Duncan Stearns turned his icy gaze upon Tolliver and smiled like a hangman after a good day's work.

"BLAM!" The scar-faced man fired his Army Colt

once, catching Tolliver between the shoulder blades and sending him flying over the neck of his horse.

"Well done, Crawford," the Scotsman had said in a husky voice. "And now, let's teach that Indian scum up ahead a little lesson," he went on, wheeling his horse around in the direction of the little band of Crows. "Give 'em hell, lads—for I want you all to be ready for the spring—when we catch up with Mister Dave Watson...."

3

WINTER SETS IN

Buffalo Bill Cody went back to his Louisa . . . reluctantly his Louisa was expecting, and it was the frontiersman's duty to be at her side. Wild Bill Hickok rode back to Hays City, Kansas, and Marcus P. Haverstraw chose to ride out once more at the side of his friend, Dave Watson, as the Kansan set out once more after Grey Thunder and Deanna MacPartland.

They left Fort Kingston the next afternoon, once the newspaperman had telegraphed his considerable copy in to his employer, the *New Orleans Picayune.* Cody and Hickok had left in the morning, and they parted from their two former trailmates with great pain and a certain amount of misgiving, which each of the frontiersman did his best to conceal from the Kansan and Marcus. But Dave Watson had seen the look in their eyes when he announced his plan, and was fully aware that Cody and Hickok, as well as Major Lanier, felt certain that they would never see him alive again. And when the pair rode through the gates of Fort Kingston, the Kansan felt a sharp pang of regret, and suddenly wished that he were riding beside them.

"Y'know, I think yer plumb loco fer stickin' with me this time, Marcus," he told the journalist as they rode over the open country to the northwest of the army post.

"Well, just because you're still trying to pick up the scent of that Cheyenne, it doesn't mean that we're going to have to rush into the middle of his camp with guns blazing and take all of those fellows on at once, now does it?"

The Kansan grinned. "No, it don't," was his terse reply.

"And besides, Marcus went on, "this is my big story—my biggest story, for that matter. I've been keeping an account of our adventures ever since we met in St. Louis, and I'll be damned if I'll let go of a story the size of this one. What we're going through is considered high adventure by millions of newspaper readers throughout this great nation of ours, I'll have you know."

"It's more fun to read about than to go through, I reckon," replied the Kansan, still grinning.

"And furthermore," Marcus continued, now grinning back at his friend, "I've been in Miss Deanna MacPartland's presence any number of times—San Francisco, for instance, and Long Island—but I've never had the pleasure of being properly introduced to her. Y'know, I've come too far and done too much not to meet the woman on whose behalf you and I have performed such a series of Herculean labors."

"Goddam, you are crazy," Dave muttered, shaking his head and smiling at his companion.

"Well, hell," Marcus told him, "if I weren't crazy, I never would have got into the newspaper business."

"We done rustled up some good copy, ol' hoss," Dave admitted. "There's no denyin' that."

"We've been lucky, as well," Marcus said, chuckling as he recalled some of the tight scrapes he and the Kansan had been in together.

Suddenly, Dave Watson's expression changed with the swiftness of a storm rolling over the plains. "Le's jus' hope our luck don't run out this time around, ol' hoss," he said flatly, casting a grim look at the newspaperman.

Marcus Haverstraw paled at the thought. "No . . . I certainly hope not," was his hesitant and sober reply.

Over the next few weeks, Dave and Marcus found themselves at the mercy of the weather, as winter set in on the plains. Their movements became severely restricted as the snows began to fall, and the distances they were able to range grew rapidly shorter. And in little more than a month's time, the two companions found themselves snowbound in a little town named Blanton, Nebraska, somewhere to the north of the Elkhorn River.

The snow came in the form of a driving blizzard, and kept the Kansan and the Connecticut reporter snowbound for a number of weeks at the house of one Alois Wofinger, a blacksmith whose wife ran a boarding house. While Blanton was a one-horse town, as Marcus referred to it, it did happen to be the junction of two stagecoach routes, hence the need for the Wolfinger boarding house. But as luck would have it, Dave and Marcus were the only two boarders present when the blizzard hit the little town in the middle of the night.

They were forced by the incredibly inclement weather to remain at their safe haven in the Wolfinger abode, and were totally grateful for such refuge, considering themselves fortunate indeed not to have been caught out on the open prairie when the blizzard swept through. And so they spent their days dreaming in front of the fireplace, and chopping wood whenever it was called for, glad of the opportunity to stretch their legs and use their muscles. Food was plentiful and delicious, since their host had amply provided for all contingencies, and his wife Bertha was an excellent cook.

Alois Wolfinger was a German by birth, one of the wave of northern Europeans who came to Nebraska in the 1850's. He was a huge man with forearms the size of a young man's thigh and broad hands with thick, knobby fingers. He had a curly brown beard and a shy grin, and was a quiet but extremely hospitable soul, a man who loved to listen to talltales and accounts of travels in strange lands. And he was utterly thrilled by the Kansan's accounts of life on the frontier, or Marcus' tales of his adventures in various great American cities.

One night, after Frau Wolfinger had cooked a most delicious meal of pot roast and potato pancakes, the three men sat in the parlor, drinking *schnapps* and gazing into the dancing flames in the fireplace. The blacksmith's wife had gone upstairs early for a change, and the men found themselves alone. She was much taken by the two guests, and usually stayed up as late as her husband, in order to hear their stories. But this evening she had been especially tired, and had gone upstairs after the nightly dessert of coffee and apple pie or *pflaumenkuchen,* the rich and tasty German plum cake.

"Boy, this here *schnapps* could knock the breath out of a bull buffalo, Alois," the Kansan told his host, grimacing as he put his glass down on the wooden floorboards.

"Ach, diss is not schtrong like ve make in Choimany," Wolfinger told Dave, reaching for the bottle and pouring the Kansan another round. "You shoult daste vot it is like in de olt country. Dere dey make *real schnapps*."

"If it gets any stronger I won't be able to drink it," observed Marcus, between sips at his glass. "The damned stuff's already burnt out all the hairs in my nose."

"Nobody's holdin' a gun to yer head an' tellin' ya to swig that stuff down, ol' hoss," the Kansan reminded the newspaperman.

"Well, all right," admitted Marcus, "But what are the alternatives? Blackberry brandy? No thank you."

"Chendlemen," Alois Wolfinger said softly, breaking the silence that had followed upon Marcus Haverstraw's last remark, "now dot mein vife is fast azleep, vhy do not ve talk of de vimmen."

"De vimmen?" repeated Dave, not understanding what the man wanted.

"Ja. De vimmen. Laties. De laties."

"*Laties?*" echoed a puzzled Kansan.

"He wants to talk about the fair sex, old boy," Marcus informed him. "Women."

"Oh, I see," said Dave, his face suddenly brightening. "Women, hah?"

"*Ja, ja!*" the German whispered eagerly, casting a surreptitious glance up at the staircase. "Now ve talk about de egzotic pragtices und mysteries of zex. All right, my goot frients?"

Dave, who had trouble understanding most of what Alois Wolfinger said, looked to Marcus for a translation.

"The mysteries of sex," the reporter told the Kansan, leering theatrically like one of the thespians he was so fond of imitating. "Mysteries and exotic practices. I suppose life must get a touch humdrum for our friend Alois, here in Blanton, and he's anxious to add a pinch of spice to his life."

"Ja, dot's de schtuff, Marcus!" the big man said, his bass whisper now grown intense. "Tell vot de vimmen is like vot you haff schlept mit."

"It seems that Alois would enjoy hearing about the young ladies whom we have met in our travels, David Lee," an amused Marcus told the Kansan.

"Well, I ain't one to kiss an' tell," Dave protested.

"Perhaps not," the newspaperman replied, holding up a hand and smiling at his friend. "But I've always been meaning to relate my curious erotic experience with Madame Yu to you, old boy. But somehow, I never quite got around to doing so." Marcus paused to take a swig of his *schnapps*. "However," he continued, shivering as the liquor went down, "since we're all snowed in together for the duration, it seems as if the perfect opportunity to disclose this most purple passage of my amorous adventures has arrived."

It was Alois Wolfinger's turn to look puzzled. "Vot you are zaying, please, Marcus? Dot fancy talk is zumtimes too confusing for me."

"Ah, to make a long story short, my dear Alois, I just told Dave here that I was about to recite a little tale of exotic sexual practices . . . something I imagine you will heartily enjoy hearing."

"Ach, ja!" the blacksmith whispered fervently. "To be sure, my frent. I vill enchoy very much. Please talk."

"All right with you, old man?" Marcus asked the Kansan.

Dave shrugged. "It's yer doin's, Marcus. So feel free to talk about whatever ya like."

"Fine. In that case, I will proceed."

"Vun moment, chendlemen," interrupted Wolfinger, reaching for the bottle of *schnapps*. "First I make like a goot hozt unt fill de glasses, *ja?*"

"That's a right good idea," agreed the Kansan, holding out his empty glass for the German to fill.

"Unt now, ve begin," the blacksmith said, once he had filled Marcus' and his own glass.

"Yes," purred Marcus, leaning over to put his glass down on the waxed and gleaming boards of the floor. "Let us begin." He sat upright on the sofa which he shared with the Kansan, rubbed his nose and then cleared his throat.

"Madame Yu is a Chinese procuress, the proprietor of a house of pleasure in the great city of New York, my dear Alois," the newspaperman explained. "Dave and I chanced to meet her when we were up there nearly half a year ago. A reporter friend tipped me to the place. So we went there. Dave made the acquaintance of a pretty little thing named Heart's Delight." Smiling, the Kansan nodded at this. "And I decided to put myself, as it were, in the capable hands of Madame Yu.

"She was a most accomplished lady, being heiress to three thousand years of Chinese sexual know-how. The celestials are a most curious race, and their researches in this field are far in advance of the discoveries of most races, I would venture to say, with the possible exception of the Hindoos."

"She knew many t'ing for de bed?" asked a hopeful Wolfinger.

"Yes, that's it exactly," Marcus replied, beaming at the blacksmith. "You understand perfectly, my dear Alois. Perfectly." He paused to bend over and pick up his glass of *schnapps,* which he sipped in silence for several moments.

"Well, what happened after little Heart's Delight conducted my friend, David Lee, to her room was that Madame Yu and I sat on her plush sofa and sipped plum wine for a bit. Suddenly this quiet spell was broken when the madam looked into my eyes—she was a most beautiful woman, with eyes as dark and shiny as polished onyx—and asked me a question.

" 'Marcus,' she said, her voice low and velvety, 'why do you choose to remain in my company, when there are so many ripe young beauties in my establishment?' "

" 'My dear Madame Yu,' I told her, gazing into those midnight orbs of hers with all the sincerity I could muster, 'why would I choose a girl when such a beautiful woman is present? As one of our occidental poets had put it, "Ripeness is all." Why partake of a green fruit when one which demonstrates the peak of ripeness is to be found at the very same table? I would be most honored should you choose to initiate me into the pleasures of the East, my dear Madame Yu.' "

"Vot means an akzidental poet?" asked Alois Wolfinger.

"Not accidental," Marcus corrected. "Occidental. It

come from a word that means 'west.' It's the opposite of 'oriental,' and means 'western,' or 'pertaining to the west.'

"Ah, to proceed," Marcus said gently as he prepared to resume his narrative, "Madame Yu said, 'You are a most gallant gentleman, Mister Haverstraw,' And then she shot me a most unmistakable look. 'And you shall have your wish,' she told me, rising from the sofa and taking me by the hand, after which she proceeded to lead me to her room."

He paused briefly, studying the face of his listeners.

"It was quite a place, that room of Madame Yu's," the newspaperman said when he resumed his tale. "Furnished with rich tapestries and silken hangings, with Persian carpets on the floor and Tiffany glass lamps hanging from silver chains. It was like something out of *The Arabian Nights*, my friends. I would never have thought to see such splendor and luxury this side of the Taj Mahal. But there it was, on Elizabeth Street, in the heart of New York City, in the good old United States of America." He grinned at Dave and Wolfinger. "As the bard said, 'There are stranger things in heaven and earth than are dreamt of in your philosophy, Horatio.'"

"Vot is a 'bart,' unt who is dis Horatio fella?" the blacksmith asked, shooting a look of appeal at the reporter.

"Sorry about that, Alois," apologized Marcus, "A bard is a poet. I was referring to our William Shakespeare. And Horatio is a character in *Hamlet*."

"*Ach, ja.* Now I zee."

"Whyn't you try to keep it simple?" the Kansan said to his friends.

Marcus grinned sheepishly and nodded. "Of course you're right, David Lee." He turned to Wolfinger. "I apologize, old boy. I'll try to keep to the essentials of the story."

"Dot I vould abbrezhiate," the blacksmith grunted into his glass of *schnapps*.

"Well, as I was saying, Madame Yu took me to her lavishly appointed room. She then poured us two glasses of plum wine, and I immediately proposed a toast.

" 'Please do, Mister Haverstraw,' she said in that dark, velvety voice of hers. Why, it gives me the shivers just to recollect the sound of it, fellows. And then I said, 'Oh, call me Marcus, Madame Yu.' And she sidled up to me and said, 'Yes-s-sss, Marcus-s-sss,' hissing like a serpent in New York's Central Park Zoo . . . at the very same time running her dexterous little hand up the inside of my trouser leg." He glanced meaningfully at the Kansan and Wolfinger in turn.

" 'I just want to make you feel comfortable, Marcus-s-sss,' she whispered in my ear, fondling the bulge which had suddenly appeared in my trousers. And I, flushing and panting at this sudden access of tenderness, proposed my little toast: 'To Madame Yu, the flower of Chinatown. To the woman who resolves all contradictions, and achieves the union of East and West.' "

"I do not undershtant dis vord, 'contra—"
"Now, hush, Alois," the newspaper said impatiently, holding up a hand as he interrupted the German. "Just keep listening, and try not to interrupt me. Just, ah, get the *feel* of what I'm telling you? All right?"

"*Ja,* I try," the German said obediently, a look of

frustration upon his face as he sank back into the overstuffed armchair which held his massive frame.

"Then, after we had drunk the toast, Madame Yu and I embraced and proceeded to get down to business. My heavens, but that woman had a talent!" he recalled fondly, smiling beatifically at his listeners. "She had the lightest touch I've ever felt in my entire life, and she did things with her mouth that would have amazed the Creole courtesans of New Orleans. I mean, that woman proceeded to engage in the most tantalizing display of oral and manual stimulation that has ever been seen upon the face of the entire North American continent, if you want my honest opinion.

"This went on for at least forty five minutes. By then I was so worked up I could have exploded like a powderkeg on a potbelly stove. But mercifully, Madame Yu chose to culminate that segment of our loveplay by engaging in the most skillful display of fellatio—" he pantomimed oral sex for the benefit of Alois Wolfinger—" of which it has ever been my pleasure to be the recipient."

"Dot vas goot, but no zo egzotic for a Shinese voman," muttered the blacksmith, disappointment showing on his face.

"Ah, but that was only the beginning, my friend. That was merely a little gesture to take the edge off of my sexual excitement, as it were: merely a little manual and oral exercise calculated to relax me." He grinned at Wolfinger and rolled his eyes. "The best is yet to come."

He paused to empty his glass of *schnapps,* which his polite host immediately refilled.

"At this point," Marcus went on, "Madame Yu began to undress." Here he rubbed his hands together. "She was an extremely full-bodied little woman, with full, dark-nippled breasts and a lustrous black muff. And when she sat on my knee, face to face with me, and rubbed that warm, thicklipped vulva of hers against me, why, my pecker shot up like a buck private snapping to attention during a dress parade.

" 'Yes-s-sss indeed, my dear Marcus-s-s-sss,' " the charming little woman hissed. 'There is much more to come. Opium. Instruments of love. And if you should so choose, my dear American friend, the technique of lovemaking known as 'beating the blossom at the back door.' There is much fruit to be plucked from the tree of pleasure before morning comes.' "

Marcus raised his hands at his sides. "Well, no man in his right mind would have cared to dispute that statement, so I just smiled eagerly and expressed the hope that morning would come none too soon. And then we went to bed."

"Uh, what about them there instruments of love?" the Kansan asked the reporter.

"Ah, yes, the instruments of pleasure," Marcus repeated melodramatically. "I'm coming to that, David Lee, old man." He turned to the blacksmith and held out his little glass. "But first I could use a wee dram of *schnapps* to wet my whistle, if it's all the same with you, my dear Alois."

"*Ja, ja!*" the German said. "Unt den you tell about de inshtruments of pleasure. *Nicht wahr?*"

"Mostly assuredly," the reporter told him, as the blacksmith refilled his glass.

"I'm mighty curious myself," the Kansan told Marcus, "to see what kinda gizmos that there Chinese madam done used on you."

"Well, opium was the first item on the agenda," Marcus said after he had taken a sip of his drink. "Madame Yu had a whole pharmacy on her bedside table. The first thing she did was to take a little pipe and pop a small pellet of opium in the thing. And then we proceeded to smoke. After that, we retired to the bed for a bit of luxurious foreplay, where I worked the gracious lady over this time."

He looked from Dave to Wolfinger. "And do you know what? In no time, I had the damnedest erection. I had one all along, you realize, but suddenly I became aware of a physical difference. My rod was very, very stiff—stiff as a poker, I tell you—and yet its nerves seemed partially anesthetized. This was most unusual, and I was able to distinguish this effect quite readily. It proved to be extremely useful, you see, gentlemen . . . for in that manner, and by pausing for an occasional pipe of opium in the rare quiet intervals, I was able to make love to Madame Yu all night long."

"Ist dies die wahrheit?" the German asked in awe. "Dis is true vot you tell us?"

"On my honor, Alois," Marcus assured him. "It's an old oriental device for prolonging one's pleasure."

"Are you sayin' ya didn't shoot yer wad all night long?" the Kansan asked skeptically.

The newspaperman shook his head. "No, I'm not. I came several times more that night. But when you consider the sheer amount of gut-wrenching, down-and-dirty, no-holds-barred fucking that the little lady and I indulged in, why, you'd have to consider it miraculous to have come so few times—or even more miraculous, to have been able to stay in the saddle so long."

Dave Watson and Alois Wolfinger both nodded, their eyes on Marcus Haverstraw's long face.

"And there were other appurtenances on the night table," Marcus informed his fascinated listeners. "There was the silver clasp, the sulphur ring, and the red powder."

"What-all's that stuff fer?" Dave asked.

"I'm coming to that," Marcus said, a trace of annoyance in his voice. "If you fellows will just simmer down and give me a chance to tell you."

The Kansan flushed and looked down at the polished floor. Alois Wolfinger busied himself with making sure that all the *schnapps* glasses were full.

"Another of Madame Yu's little tricks was the silver clasp, sort of a ring or band that clamps around the base of the pecker. And what it does is cut off the flow of blood from that organ to the body, thereby maintaining a full erection. I've, ah, heard of fellows using a rubber band to achieve the same purpose in this country. And she told me that the Japanese call the silver clasp the 'pleasure ring.' I ah, suppose such a practice could be dangerous if indulged in regularly—you know, it could give rise to lesions and ulceration of the penis—but it admirably served its purpose that night, and in addition to the opium prevented me from ending the night too soon. We really fucked heroically, gents. I was a wreck for the next few days."

The Kansan nodded. "So that's why you was off yer feed, hah? I never could figger that one out."

"My balls felt as swollen as bagpipes," Marcus told him. "And my pecker felt as if it had been flayed." He shook his head. "No, my friends. That is definitely not something one would do every night. Not on your life."

"Dot vould be too much of a goot t'ing, *nah ja?*" said the blacksmith, grinning shyly at Marcus Haverstraw.

"Most definitely," the reporter agreed. "She also had me put on the sulphur ring, which is a device that is bound to the penis, around the neck of the glans, where it is most sensitive. It shields the corona and the frenum—uh, excuse me," he said holding up a hand, "the underside of the head, and just below. That's the seat of the most intense feeling for a man. The sulphur is used like alum—that is to say it's used as an astringent, to tighten and constrict the walls of the vagina, there by increasing friction and making the act of love more pleasurable. Another use for the stuff is as a resolvent, in order to absorb some of the copious secretions from the little lady's honeypot at the same time."

"By Gad," Dave murmured, "the way you was trussed-up with them gizmos, you musta looked like a knight in armor."

"Oh, that wasn't all," Marcus casually informed him. "I haven't told you fellows about the 'hedgehog.'"

"Hedgehog?" croaked the Kansan. "What in hell's all this got to do with a damn hedgehog?"

"Not the actual animal, old man. It's another oriental device, a ring studded with soft bristles or feathers, or sometimes even blunt India rubber points. Over here we call 'em 'French ticklers.'"

"Unt vot for is dot?" asked a sweating Wolfinger, leaning forward to catch the newspaperman's reply.

"The 'tickler' and other related gadgets are supposed to increase tension and excitement in a woman's lower parts," Marcus explained, "so that she will undergo a considerable number of violent and powerful spasms . . . which, in turn, will make her delirious with rapture and eventually cause her to swoon. That's the theory."

"How 'bout the practice?" asked the Kansan. "Did it work with ol' Madame Yu?"

The newspaperman raised his eyebrows as he started at his friend. "To tell you the truth, it was hard to tell objectively, I mean. Y'see, Madame Yu seemed to be enjoying everything so much that it was hard to accurately gauge the effects of any individual action or method." He sighed and shrugged his shoulders. "I was most flattered to have put her into such a high state of excitement," he went on. "But then my newspaperman's skepticism reasserted itself, and I recalled that it was also her job to simulate pleasure for the benefit of the customers. So I never could really tell what was real and what was not." He shook his head. "And to this day, I don't know. So help me, God."

"But vot you did mit her?" the blacksmith asked. "Vot happened mit all dis eqvipment dot you vas vearing?"

"Ah, well, we played around a bit more, between sips of plum wine and tokes on that little opium pipe of hers," Marcus told Wolfinger. "I was above her, probing her opening with my rod, and sliding it up and down between those thick nether lips, until she writhed and moaned beneath me, begging me to penetrate her.

" 'What a bearded delight is that most magnificent of members,' " she crooned to me, smiling wickedly and gazing fondly at my private parts through half-lidded eyes. "It's, ah, very flattering to have to and a woman talk that way in bed, my friends, let me tell you. It seems that the oriental women—or at least the courtesans among them—tend to do that to the men. And it certainly gets a fellow worked up.

" 'Oh, spare me the attack of such a great and vigorous member,' " Madame Yu went on, all the time arching her pelvis toward me. So naturally, I went to it with the utmost ardor, stroking and thrusting hundreds of times, while she wriggled and sighed and gasped beneath me, sounding as if she were about to expire any minute." Marcus leaned over and picked up his glass of *schnapps*.

"After a while," he continued once he had drunk, "I came out and rolled over, just waiting to catch my second wind.

" 'Put the red powder on your lotus stalk, my dear Marcus-s-s-sss,' " she whispered, reaching over to the bedside table and picking up a small, circular container made of carved ivory, which she opened and proceeded to hand to me. 'Whatever you say, my celestial delight,' I replied, more than eager to comply with her intsructions, since she had already been giving me the ride of my life."

"What was in that there red powder?" Dave Watson asked the newspaperman.

"As I recollect, it was composed of varying amounts of ginger, pepper, mustard, cinnamon . . . and I don't know what else—all irritants intended to make the mucous membranes of the vagina swell. This causes the vaginal canal to get very tight around the penis, affording a hell of a lot of friction and therefore pleasure to both parties, according to my instructress."

"Vas is dis vochinel ganal?" a bewildered Wolfinger asked as he refilled his glass.

"The inside of her thing," Marcus said flatly, eager to resume his narrative.

"And then she told me that she was going to put some 'medicine between her thighs,' in order to further sensitize her 'chicken's tongue' and 'frog's mouth.' " Marcus grinned and sat back in his chair, waiting for the response which he knew would inevitably follow his last words.

"Shicken's tongk? Frok's mout'?" gasped Alois Wolfinger.

"I don't know what the hell yer takin' 'bout," Dave Watson told Marcus.

The journalist chuckled at this. "The chicken's tongue is the clitoris," he said, illustrating his explanation for the benefit of the German. "And the frog's mouth is the opening of the vagina. That's what the Chinese call 'em."

"Vunce in Choimany, ven I vas youngk," said Alois Wolfinger, "I knew dis girl who hat zuch a big bussy dot I t'ought of a cow bussy." He made a gesture with his hands.

"There, you see?" Marcus told the other two men. "The animal analogies are common, and not just the creation of the Chinese. Well, there we were: I had just applied the red powder and Madame Yu had, as she so quaintly put it, applied the medicine 'between her thighs.' And then she leered at me and whispered, saying wouldn't I prefer to spread her legs, and tie her feet to the bedposts." He held out his hands. "It seemed like a good idea at the time, boys." He flashed Dave and the blacksmith an apologetic smile.

"So I tied her legs to the bedposts with a scarlet ribbon, and she lay there before me, her portal wide open and the purple valley beyond it clearly visible. Damn me, if this wasn't rather exciting! So I came over and thrust myself inside her. 'Don't be afraid to move violently, my darling,' she whispered, darting her tongue into my ear. The woman seemed to enjoy a high degree of pain in her intimate relations," Marcus explained.

"Y'know, that was something I hadn't thought about very much until Dave and I ran into a bunch of wild Russians on Long Island's Montauk peninsula a few months back," he told Wolfinger. "There I had a little bedroom encounter with a very passionate gypsy singer who wanted me to flog her with a blasted bullwhip. But at any rate, it's opened my eyes. Apparently pleasure comes in many forms. That's what I've been led to conclude, these days."

"Darn tootin'," the Kansan agreed.

"So I began to let Madame Yu have it, alternating long strokes with short strokes, hard strokes with soft strokes, until she was gibbering beneath me, and pleading for me to finish her off.

" 'It is time,' she told me, 'for the monk to strike the gong. Thrust yourself with in me as deeply and vigorously as you can, until you make contact with the stamen of the flower within.'

"And, by God, I did," Marcus told his listeners, "and the sulphur ring broke open. Madame Yu howled like a coyote and drew back, shuddering from head to toe. And after that she closed her eyes and fell back onto the bed, sighing as she did. I thought she was going to expire—the Japanese call that 'the sweet death.' But no, she gradually came around, and then proceeded to work me over once again with that incredibly skilled mouth of hers. This finally caused me to have an earthshaking climax, and I, too, nearly expired." He smiled at the Kansan and Wolfinger. "And after that, we spent more hours in amorous dalliance."

"Judas Priest!" murmured Dave Watson. "No wonder you was so tuckered out when we left that Chinese cat-house!"

"It was a most unusual—and a most exhausting—experience," was Marcus' reply.

"Gosh," said Alois Wolfinger in a hushed voice. "Dot vas egzitingk!"

"Whenever I hook up with my old pal, Dave, life is rarely dull. Remind me to tell you of our adventures in Virginia City and San Francisco, Alois. He and I have had pretty exciting times."

"*Ja!*" the blacksmith told him, nodding his head eagerly as he rose from his seat. "You bet I do dot. But now I go into de kitchen unt make for us some sammiches."

"Well, if I had to be snowbound somewhere in Nebraska," Marcus told the Kansan, "I don't suppose that I could have found a better place. Old Alois isn't much on charm and fancy talk, but he's the perfect host."

"I reckon," Dave replied, nodding glumly. "But I wish we could git the hell outta here an' ride on."

"You're worrying about Deanna again, aren't you, old man?"

The Kansan nodded his head again. "I reckon I am. I jus' can't keep myself from wond'rin' how she's doin'." He sighed. "I mean, she's in the hands of one wild sum'bitch. From all we heard so far, that damn Grey Thunder is a real bad-ass."

"Yes," Marcus Haverstraw agreed. "But just because he's killed and scalped any number of men, it doesn't necessarily follow that he abuses women."

The Kansan shot him a dark look. "He ain't keepin' Deanna jus' so she'll keep his tent clean."

It was the newspaperman's turn to sigh. "I know," he said wearily, looking down at the polished hardwood floor. "But I've learned one thing about your Deanna since we've been looking for her, David Lee. And what I've learned is that the little girl can take care of herself. She's of the type that survives, my friend. So don't get so upset."

"But she's sharin' a tent with that goddam buck!" the Kansan protested.

"That doesn't change things," Marcus said sternly, his eyes suddenly flashing as they met Dave Watson's. "What's important is that you get her back." His eyes narrowed. "And that's *all* that is important. Nothing else matters. We're on the frontier, with an Indian uprising in the making. Just pray to God that you get her back."

"Yer right," Dave agreed, forcing a smile as he looked into his friend's eyes. "Nothin' else matters much alongside of that."

"It's going to clear soon," Marcus said reassuringly. "Then we can get out of here."

The Kansan said nothing, just nodded his head tiredly as he picked up his gunbelt from the seat beside him, took the big Walker Colt out of the holster and began to polish its long barrel with a rag.

"We'll find her," Marcus assured him. "And then we'll figure out how to rescue her."

Dave Watson nodded, his attention seemingly focused upon the gun in his hand. At that moment Alois

Wolfinger entered the room, bearing a big platter containing bread, ham, roast pork and cheese.

"I'm gon' have to kill that sum'bitch," the Kansan said slowly, deliberately, looking up from the Walker Colt to stare at the German.

The blacksmith went white in the face, and his hands shook as he put the platter down upon the floor before his two guests.

"Now, don't you git riled up none, Alois," Dave said gently. "I ain't referrin' to nobody present at the moment."

"Ooof!" wheezed the big German. "Dot is a relief. I zaw you mit dot gun, unt I got shcairt."

"He's referring to Grey Thunder, the Cheyenne who ran off with Deanna MacPartland."

"Ach, dot vun!" the blacksmith grunted angrily. *"Was fur ein schweinhund!"*

"I reckon I got to plug 'im," the Kansan said in a matter-of-fact tone of voice.

"Don't you, ah, think we might have a chance to, ah, ransom Deanna?" Marcus asked anxiously.

Dave shook his head. "When an Injun gits it in his head that somethin's his, an' he wants to keep it, ain't no way in hell you gon' git him to part with it." His eyes blazed as they met those of the reporter. "An' Deanna ain't the kind of woman men want to give away."

"You vill haff to kill him, for zure?" Alois Wolfinger asked in a hushed voice.

"I reckon," was the reply. "I don't figger he's about to give Deanna up fer nothin'. He already been callin' her his 'golden woman,' ain't he?" the Kasan said, a trace of anger in his voice, a voice which had grown suddenly husky. He shook his head. "Uh-uh. I figger the only way we're gon' settle this to ever'body's satisfaction is when either him or me's planted six foot under the ground."

4

INDIANS

The Kansan and Marcus left Alois Wolfinger's house two days later, and rode out of the small Nebraska town of Blanton with the wind at their back, heading south. The pressure of the advancing winter had left its mark on Dave Watson's determination as well as upon the land, and even the resolute Kansan was forced to turn back from his quest. He had become convinced that there would be no locating Deanna MacPartland until the spring, and it was with a heavy heart that he and Marcus had decided to return to Hays City.

Duncan Stearns was making his way back there as well, and when the two men met, there was sure to be trouble. And the worst part of it, as far as the Kansan was concerned, was that he was still unaware that the big Scotsman was out hunting him. When and if the two men encountered each other in the streets of Hays City, lead would surely fly; and the fact that Stearns rode at the head of ten bloodthirsty desperadoes did not bode well for Dave Watson, who was presently accompanied by only one man, the reporter Marcus P. Haverstraw.

The "Buffalo Soldiers" of the Tenth Cavalry rested secure behind the stockade which defended Fort Kingston, welcoming the harsh weather, which brought them a respite in their almost constant pursuit of the hostiles who presently flooded the lower section of the U.S. Army's vast Department of the Missouri. The post was preoccupied for the moment with spit-and-polish, and other makework schemes created to occupy the time and energies of soldiers at camp, for it would not be until the arrival of spring that the horse soldiers and their infantry counterparts would sally forth in full strength once more, resuming their all-but-impossible mission of confronting the hostile tribes, protecting the settlers and merchants, and generally keeping the peace on the Great Plains.

The tribes had met in the late fall for their annual rituals and conclaves; and now, in the heart of winter, they had long since dispersed, breaking up once more into their constituent bands, each going off to its own winter camp. The lean times were upon the land, and the Indians who ranged it had retired to their places of shelter, in order to await the coming of spring.

Behind one of the bluffs that tower over the Loup River, Grey Thunder and the Cheyennes who followed him had made camp for the winter. Their Sioux and Arapaho allies had gone back to their own people, intending to rejoin the band once the warm weather had come, and in consequence of this, the encampment was considerably smaller than it had been a few months earlier.

Grey Thunder, his male relatives, and friends sat upon buffalo robes in their teepees and smoked their pipes, talking of old times and planning their strategy for the spring, when they would once more attack the hated whites who had encroached upon their hunting grounds, killing all the men and burning all the houses and ranches to the ground.

The raid on Duncan Stearns' ranch had given the band many good horses, the best of which Grey Thunder had taken for his own, although as a Cheyenne, he soon gave most of them away to the less prosperous members of his group. But this prize had given the warrior pause, and it had become his dream that he might, in another year or two, return to the Cheyenne with a string of fine horses, offering them to the peace chief of his people. And if they were accepted, Grey Thunder would vow to follow the Cheyenne Way, and then be readmitted to full membership in the tribe, having explained his guilt and proven himself ready to be rehabilitated. Exile was the punishment for murder among the Cheyenne, and among that close-knit and socially conscious tribe, it was the worst of all possible penalties. And yet, at the same time, this grave sentence, like some American Indian Pandora's box, carried within itself, in addition to its freight of woes, the hope of ultimate forgiveness and acceptance.

This was Grey Thunder's dream: to be reunited with his people, to hunt and fight for them, to win honor and glory in battle, and to provide for those among them less fortunate than he. There were no greater people than the Cheyenne: He had been taught this from birth, and he believed it with all his heart.

Golden Woman, his fair prize, lived in the warrior's teepee and slept with him at night. He was not in the least interested in whom she had been before he carried her off: what mattered to Grey Thunder was that his new woman learn the ways of his people. And Deanna MacPartland realized this as well, knowing that her best hope for eventual rescue or escape lay in her adoption of Indian ways. Thereby lay her salvation, and she sat in silence beside the wives of the Cheyenne, as they taught her how to scrape hides, erect a teepee, and prepare the daily meals, as well as a host of other things.

She learned the Cheyenne language as well, totally accepting her present predicament, determined to make the most of her captivity. Fair and delicate though she appeared to be, Deanna MacPartland was a woman of great flexibility and resourcefulness. And in her heart of hearts, she kept her love alive for Dave Watson, even though the last she had seen of the Kansan was when he lay crippled and suffering upon the hard, sandy earth of the easternmost point of Long Island, more than a thousand miles away from the tents of the Cheyenne. But she never lost hope of seeing her beloved once more, and was resigned to find him again, no matter how long it might take to do so.

The Kansan had crossed a continent to return to her, and after she had been kidnapped by John Hartung, had traveled from the port of New Orleans to New York City in search of Deanna. He had sworn to be true to her. This oath had been taken when they made love in the very shadow of death, and Deanna knew full well that Dave Watson would continue to search for her while life remained in his body. On her part, she had sworn a great oath to herself; she would wait for him, come hell or high water. Crippled or whole, it made no difference.

So she became one with the Cheyenne of Grey Thunder's outlaw band, resigned to her fate, but at the same time alert to the possibility of a sudden reversal, and wholly determined to take any reasonable chance for escape that should happen to come her way. For the moment she was content to be Golden Woman; but at the first chance of escape, she would once more become Deanna MacPartland. She did her best to live as the Kansan had taught her: *one day at a time*. This was the great gift that her lover had given her, and it freed her from unnecessary worry about the future. She had decided to live in the present, to stay in the moment; and when tomorrow came, she would deal with it accordingly. Once she had been able to accept this sage advice and put it to use, Deanna had found herself freed of a great many fears which had formerly plagued her. *"To everything there is a season,"* it said in the Bible, and she was beginning to understand the great wisdom which reposed in that simple pronouncement.

Furthermore, in this spirit of acceptance, Deanna did not feel guilty or soiled whenever she slept with the Cheyenne warrior. She had little or no choice, and her life was at stake. Dave Watson would understand. She knew that, for he had first encountered her in a brothel in the town of Hawkins Fork, Kansas. Their love ran far deeper than that. Deanna recalled what Dave had told her once, one of his beloved Uncle Ethan's favorite sayings: *All things are pure to the pure in heart*. And that was one fact of which Deanna MacPartland had absolutely no doubt: She loved the Kansan as purely and unselfishly as it was possible for her to love anyone. She had given herself to him completely, and never wavered in her love or devotion from that day on.

They would be reunited once again: Deanna never doubted that. She trusted in Almighty God to sustain them both in all their tribulations. Both she and the Kansan placed their trust in God, believing that would enable them to bear their burdens with grace and humility throughout the span of their lives. The Kansan was a simple, honest man who stood up for what he believed to be right, and Deanna MacPartland drew strength from this, and had vowed to keep faith with the man she loved. This sustained her in the dark and bitter period of her captivity.

Duncan Stearns was smiling grimly as he rode back to Hays City, Kansas. The reason for this was that he had recently hatched a scheme that was far more ambitious and larger in scope than the one which had originally sent him out on the plains, aflame with a desire to avenge himself upon the Kansan. He was smiling because his new scheme accomodated both the killing of Dave Watson *and* the rescue of Deanna MacPartland.

The young bucks of the tribes were out for blood, as demonstrated by recent events. The Scotsman intended to make good use of the general unrest on the frontier. He had learned about Grey Thunder's band, and now knew who was in possession of Deanna MacPartland. Duncan Stearns intended to kill the Cheyenne brave, as well as Dave Watson, in order to have the blonde beauty who fascinated him all to himself. To this end, Stearns intended to stir up popular feeling against the Indians, which would not be hard, he reminded himself, in light of Grey Thunder's depredations.

Let the troops of the U.S. Army blunder around like

the fools they were, Duncan Stearns thought scornfully. What he would do, after a winter's work rousing the local settlers and ranchers in his part of the country, and once the spring had come, was to ride out at the head of a great band of armed men and sweep the plains, settling the hash of whatever bunch of savages happened to cross his path. And he would go out with his Hays City bully-boys at the head of this small army—those desperadoes who would gun down their own fathers for hire—stopping at nothing until he confronted Grey Thunder and rescued Deanna MacPartland . . . and secured for himself the nomination for governor of the sovereign state of Kansas.

He was out for big game now. Stearns would turn his hired killers loose on Dave Watson and all those who were unfortunate enough to ride with him; and at the same time, the Scotsman would be at the head of a group of citizens, leading them with the high purpose of making the country safe for white settlement. He would have the woman he lusted after, to boot: Stearns knew that if the Kansan were out of the way, he would be unchallenged when it came to the fair little woman whom the late John Hartung had sold to him.

And who knew? With a little luck, Dave Watson might even return to Hays City. Stearns chuckled at the thought, and turned to stare at Crawford, the scar-faced, curly-headed desperado who had become his hireling. He paid the man well, and in return, Crawford was willing to do any black deed Stearns should ask of him. The Scotsman was pleased with his lethal new associate, for it meant that he could now settle a score and keep his hands clean at the same time. This last item was extremely important to a man who enter-tained hopes of sitting in the governor's mansion in Topeka.

Duncan Stearns had been born in Inverness, in the Scottish Highlands, and had been brought to the United States as a boy. He grew up in Kansas, during the wild and woolly times of the Abolition-Pro Slavery riots, and the attendant vendettas and border raids. His father had been killed in one of those raids into Missouri, being a staunch abolitionist, and young Duncan was orphaned at the early age of eleven. But the boy went out on his own, determined not to end up like his pious and good-hearted father, and soon grew into a man who cared for no one, a man who was hard as nails.

He was big and powerfully-built, with the strength and stamina of an ox. He knew early on what he wanted from life, and had resolved to let nothing stop him from getting it. He had brawled and he had killed; and by the time he was thirty-five, Duncan Stearns had become one of the most powerful men in the entire state of Kansas. His connections (thanks in part to the efforts of his canny Scots partner, Bert Freckleton) reached all the way to Topeka. If he had his way, they would one day reach as far as Washington, D.C. And in this troubled time on the American frontier, Duncan Stearns was certain that he had hit upon a strategem which would, once it had proven its effectiveness, allow him to write his own ticket.

In the meantime he would retire to Hays City and make his plans. Then, when the snows had melted and the icy winds from the north had ceased to blow, Duncan Stearns would ride out at the head of his small army—a ride he was sure would ultimately take him all the way to Topeka to the governor's mansion.

The Kansan and Marcus Haverstraw were once again forced off the trail by the weather, and this time they spent the long and snowbound days in a small town just across the Colorado state line, at a point where it touched Nebraska. The name of the town was Red Rock, and Dave Watson and his journalist friend stayed there for several weeks, living in the large two-storied building which housed the Red Rock Saloon, where the two men took their meals and spent the greater part of their time.

"Down in the valley, valley so lo-ow,
Hang your head over,
Hear the wind blow...."

As the words of that most mournful song drifted across the barroom, Dave Watson was swept away from the present by a wave of memory. That song had been sung by Ace Landry, the desperado who gunned down the Kansan's father. And that act had launched Dave on the odyssey of vengeance and adventure which had not yet ended and would not end until he had been safely reunited with Deanna MacPartland.

"Write me a letter,
Send it by mail,
And back it in care of
The Barbourville jail...."

Sometimes it felt as if his searching would never come to an end. And when his spirits were at their lowest ebb, the Kansan imagined himself kin to the Flying Dutchman, that legendary skipper who was condemned to sail the seas for all eternity. It seemed to

Dave Watson, as he sat at a table in the Red Rock Saloon and listened to the bass voice of the man at the upright piano, that he, too, was fated to wander forever. The only difference, he told himself, was that his wanderings had been accomplished on horseback, on dry land. But it seemed as if he would be forever riding in and out of towns, never able to settle down, never able to live like other folks. . . .

"I've just had some news of Bill Cody, old fellow," Marcus Haverstraw said cheerfully as he returned from the bar, holding a bottle of whiskey and two shot glasses.

The Kansan looked up at the newspaperman. "What's that son of a gun up to these days?" he asked.

"Well, it seems that he went home," Marcus told him, "back to that little prairie cabin of his near Fort McPherson, Nebraska. He's living there now with his wife and daughter, and two of his sisters."

Dave nodded. "The man shore 'nuf takes care of his fam'ly, don't he?"

Marcus beamed at him. "Speaking of family, my dear friend, I have the great pleasure to inform you that Mrs. Cody has again successfully been delivered of an offspring."

"Bet'cha it's another girl," the Kansan drawled, recalling how desperately young Buffalo Bill had wanted a son.

The reporter for the *New Orleans Picayune* shook his head. "Not on your life. It was a boy, and Bill's named him Kit Carson Cody."

"Judas Priest, ain't that a fancy name!" exclaimed the Kansan.

"Oh, he idolizes the little fellow," Marcus went on.

"And I understand that he's so overjoyed at having a son that's he's making a thorough pest out of himself. They say he hauls just about anyone he can get his hands on into the nearest saloon and then proceeds to regale him with detailed and endless reports on little Kit's behavior."

"You didn't know none of this stuff when you went up fer whiskey," the Kansan said, cocking an eye at the newspaperman. "How in the hell did you learn so much 'bout Bill Cody an' his fam'ly in such a short time?"

Marcus grinned at him. "Remember, if you will, David Lee, that gathering information is my profession. I, ah, happened to overhear a stagecoach driver who just came here from Fort McPherson, and I pumped him for some more information regarding Buffalo Bill *and* Wild Bill."

"How's Wild Bill doin'?" Dave asked.

The reporter shook his head. "The fellow didn't say. I suppose he didn't stick around Hays City too long." He shrugged. "These frontier types like to wander."

"They shore enough do," the Kansan agreed.

"What I also heard about Bill Cody," Marcus Haverstraw went on, "was that he recently harbored a fugitive from justice at his place."

"You mean someone who done run afoul of the law?" Dave asked, pouring himself and the newspaperman a drink of whiskey.

"Yes, indeed," was Marcus' reply. "Billy Thompson, who is the younger brother of one Ben Thompson, a gambler and gunfighter of some repute in Texas, apparently was involved in an altercation with one of the townspeople of Ogallala, Nebraska. Young Billy shot the man, and was promptly captured by the infuriated populace, who intended to lynch him without benefit of a jury trial."

"That's the way it's usually done," the Kansan deadpanned.

"Ben Thompson got wind of this, and promptly recruited the aid of a buffalo hunter he used to pal around with in his younger days. The man is presently sheriff of the county in your home state where Dodge City is located."

Dave muttered the name of the county as Marcus paused to knock back his drink.

"Masterson was the fellow's name," Marcus told the Kansan, resuming his tale as he thumped the shot glass down upon the table top. "Bat Masterson. Ben Thompson had once saved the man's life, and now he was calling in the debt. He asked Bat Masterson to save his kid brother from being lynched at the hands of the angry citizens of Ogallala."

"So Masterson went there and discovered that Billy Thompson was laid up in a hotel, where he was being kept under armed guard. Bat Masterson, who seems to be quite a resourceful fellow, bribed the guard and managed to get Billy on a westbound train which left at midnight. They got off at North Platte. And who should be waiting for them there?"

"Bill Cody?"

"Right you are. He had brought a spring wagon to the station, and from there he took Bat Masterson and Billy Thompson to his little ranch house. Billy stayed on at the place for about a month, leaving only a few days ago, when his wound had healed."

"Why'd Cody do it?" the Kansan asked.

"It seems that he's a friend of this Bat Masterson fellow."

"Oh," Dave said quietly, nodding his head.

"I guess you could say," Marcus told him, "that it's an example of the 'code of the West'."

Dave nodded again. "I reckon you could say that, ol' hoss." He picked up his glass and emptied it.

"Any word on our pal Grey Thunder?" he asked as he put down the glass and poured two more drinks.

Marcus shook his head. "The winter seems to have given the quietus to all Indian activity on the plains. But I did hear about your other good friend, Duncan Stearns."

"Duncan Stearns," the Kansan murmured, scratching the two-days' worth of stubble on his chin. "Y'know, I plumb fergot about that sum'bitch."

"Well, it appears that he hasn't forgotten about *you,* old man. The word from Hays City is that he's out for blood. And more than that, he's stirring people up against the Indians. I understand he intends to lead a big force of civilians out on the plains, once it warms up."

"Wild Bill told me Stearns ain't the man to forgive nor forget. Them Injuns done burned his ranch to the ground and took Deanna from him. An' I done whipped his ass—" The Kansan looked at Marcus and grinned a wry grin. "With a li'l help from you, ol' hoss."

Marcus winced at the memory, and unconsciously flexed his right hand. "As you say, he's one tough son of a bitch."

"Yep," agreed Dave. "An' now he's a-lookin' to

even up the score . . . with me *and* the Injuns." The Kansan's eyes narrowed. "Why, I'll bet that sum'bitch is set on gittin' Deanna back, as well!"

"You think so?" the reporter asked.

"Mebbe. If he's as determined as Bill says."

Marcus Haverstraw sighed and looked down his pump-handle nose at his friend. "That means yet another obstacle in our path, old man."

"Mebbe," the Kansan replied in a cold, quiet voice. "An' I reckon it means I got to save a bullet or two fer that big redheaded sum'bitch." He reached for his glass and listened to the mellifluous voice of the piano player, as the man repeated the mournful song which he had played only a short while ago:

"Down in the valley, valley so lo-ow,
Hang your head over,
Hear the wind blow. . . ."

The news that Duncan Stearns would soon lead an armed force over the plains gave a new urgency to the Kansan's quest, and he and Marcus rode out of Red Rock two days later, as soon as the snow had stopped falling.

They had provisioned themselves before leaving, and it was Dave's intention to ride northeast, toward the Platte River in Nebraska, in the hopes of picking up some information as to Grey Thunder's whereabouts. The Plains Indians camped by rivers or creeks, in places which were heavily sheltered: The Kansan knew that by virtue of his adoption by the Pawnee tribe. The Indians had stores of food for their meager winter meals, but were always in need of a source of fresh water.

The Cheyenne ranged over a vast amount of territory in the American West, and the Kansan had no idea of where Grey Thunder's band of hostiles was actually camped. He was merely playing a hunch. But he could no longer sit idly by and wait for the coming of spring; no, Duncan Stearns had changed all that. And when the weather changed, why, all hell would break loose; he was absolutely certain of that. The plains would be aflame with Indian raids and white reprisals, with gunfire and burning ranches. And the earth would shudder to the thunder of hoofbeats, as the various contending parties galloped across the prairie on their errands of death and destruction.

Grey Thunder, Stearns, the United States Cavalry—all would be out in force, come spring, the Kansan reminded himself. And more likely, the tribes would be roused by the white reprisals against the young Indian hostiles who had chosen to go on the warpath. At that time, the frontier would see the beginnings of an out-and-out war.

Dave Watson knew that if he did not locate Deanna MacPartland before the coming of spring, his task would be greatly complicated, and the number of his enemies would be greatly increased. And so he and Marcus Haverstraw set out in the heart of winter, in mid-January 1871, after having spent more than a month in the Colorado town of Red Rock. The new year had been greeted with discouragement and uncertainty on the Kansan's part, but as he rode out once more, it was with renewed hope and courage. He prayed that he would finally be reunited with the woman he loved; prayed that his years of wandering and hardship would finally come to an end. And he prayed as he always had, asking the Almighty for serenity, courage and wisdom:

*"God grant me the serenity to accept the things I
   cannot change; the courage to change the things I
   can; and the wisdom to know the difference.
   Amen."*

The weather was brutally cold by the time the two men neared the Platte, and even the determined Kansan was forced to admit that they would not be able to endure much more of it. It was with great reluctance that he suggested to the newspaperman that they retire to the nearest town. General Winter had swept the field once again.

"You had enough, ol' hoss?" Dave asked, squinting across the campfire at Marcus, who sat huddled against a boulder, covered by a blanket.

The newspaperman sniffled and wiped his nose before he spoke. "I wouldn't mind coming in out of the cold for a bit, I can tell you that. Not that I'm ready to give up, you understand."

Dave smiled at this, his chapped lips smacking painfully as he did. Beyond their little shelter of clustered boulders not far from the banks of the Platte, the icy winter wind howled like a fiend from hell. The sky looked dark as a judge's robe, and intermittent flashes of lightning could be seen to the northwest, with thunder rumbling ominously a short time after it. Before long a storm would break, and there was not much time to seek shelter before it did.

"We got to find us some cover, Marcus," Dave told his friend. " 'Cause there's gon' be one hell of a downpour any minute. Look at them damn clouds."

"Where shall we go?" the reporter asked.

"Up that-a-way," the Kansan told him, pointing toward the bluffs which overlooked the river less than a mile ahead. "Looks to me like there's some caves amongst them cliffs. That seems to be the most likely spot for us to shelter. An' if they ain't roomy enough fer the horses, we can still tie the animals up under the cover of some of them there big rock ledges. C'mon, let's make tracks."

Marcus spooned down the last of his pinto beans and chased them with the remaining morsel of the hardtack which constituted the rest of his supper. Then, as the Kansan stood up and began to put out the fire, the newspaperman drank the last of his strong black coffee.

A few moments later the two companions had completely packed their gear, and were leading their horses down the rocky slope that led to the near bank of the River Platte. When they reached the riverbank, the pair mounted their horses and made their way over to the cliffs, walking the animals most of the way because of the soft and rocky soil there.

By the time that Dave and Marcus approached the towering cliffs, the storm had broken. Lightning flashed, searing the stone face of the cliff walls with its blinding intensity, and thunder boomed like field artillery aimed at a city under siege. The rain pelted down in sheets, blurring the shape of objects and the demon wind howled and whined and whistled like a concert of damned souls.

The Kansan, leading his horse now, with Marcus Haverstraw behind him doing the same, inched his way up the slope which led from the bank of the Platte ascending to the caves in the cliffs that loomed above the storm-lit river. The ascent was long and arduous, for the gradient of the slope increased rapidly as the two men climbed. Both were now soaked to the skin, and cursing as they slipped on the slick rock surfaces, or whenever their horses bolted, the beasts frightened by the sudden flashes of lightning and the attendant cannonades of thunder.

"Up there, Marcus," the Kansan called out over his shoulder to the newspaperman, pointing up ahead to his right. "See that openin' there? That one looks plenty big enough to fit us an' our horses."

"Anything, I'll settle for anything," moaned the reporter, grunting as he tugged at the reins of his horse, impatient to have the frightened beast follw him up the precipitious slope. "I'd lodge in a bear's asshole just to get out of this blasted storm!"

The Kansan laughed as he turned his head and peered into the mouth of the big cave which stood almost sixty feet above the river. But he wasn't laughing when his eyes adjusted to the gloom of the place and he saw what awaited him within.

"Oh, my God!" Marcus Haverstraw gasped as he came up alongside Dave Watson. "Oh, my God. *Indians!*"

5

IN THE PAWNEE CAMP

Marcus Haverstraw's anguished cry still rang in his ears as the Kansan stood at the mouth of the big cave above the River Platte and slowly raised his hands in the air. The Connecticut journalist did the same, after casting an anxious eye on his trailmate. But Dave Watson did not respond; he was busy studying the occupants of the cave.

A small fire burned at the far end of the rock shelter, and its low, flickering light outlined the forms of the six men who stood facing the Kansan and Marcus Haverstraw. Since the six were backlighted, and the cave was extremely dark, owing to its large size, it took several moments for Dave Watson's eyes to adjust to the gloom and pick out the significant details of this sudden encounter. And as he squinted into the darkness, the Kansan was not encouraged, for he, like Marcus before him, had already discerned from the silhouettes of the cave's occupants that they were Indians. That first intelligence did not do much to cheer him, for the plains were alive with hostiles, and the odds were high against the possibility of running into a band of braves who belonged to a tribe friendly to the white man.

Dave Watson was fully aware of this grim likelihood as he squinted into the depths of the cave. What he saw as his eyes began to make out details in the gloom was not at all encouraging. The six braves were all carrying firearms, and each man held his weapon at the ready, trained on Marcus and the Kansan. He noticed that the Indians were all extraordinarily well-armed. Two of them held Army Colts in their hands, and the remaining four leveled at him what appeared to be Spencer repeating rifles. The Spencers were highly prized for their great firepower; they were the rifles, the Kansan suddenly recalled, which had enabled Major George A. Forsyth and his band of fifty men to withstand the massed attacks of nearly a thousand Cheyenne, Sioux and Arapaho warriors at Arikaree Creek. That great stand, in which Dave and his blood-brother Soaring Hawk had participated, had become known as the Battle of Beecher's Island and one of its results had been the death of the great Cheyenne war-chief, Roman Nose. It was even possible, among all the bullets fired at the Chief as he and his horsemen charged Forsyth's position, that those from the rifles of the Kansan and his Pawnee companion had actually brought the Cheyenne down. As he stood in the mouth of the cave, hands held in the air, Dave Watson saw that fateful charge again in his mind's-eye, and relived it for an instant. . . .

There he was again, on that small island in the center of the dry creek, reloading his Spencer rifle, with Soaring Hawk at his side and a number of Indian scouts and trappers crouched behind rocks or hidden in the dry, brown grass that covered their position. The late Jack Poole was there, as well as several other veteran scouts such as Eli Zigler, Sigman Schlesinger, Henry Tucker, Pierre Trudeau, Jack Stillwell and Jack Donovan. And Major George A. Forsyth was there as well, in pain but still in command, despite the two wounds he had taken in the battle. So cool a hand was the former colonel in the Union Army that when help finally arrived, after a nine-day siege, the rescuers found George Forsyth reading from Charles Dickens' David Copperfield *as they rode in.*

It was noon of the second day, and the sun was high overhead. Roman Nose, the warchief whom the Cheyennes believed to be invulnerable, took his place at the head of a mounted Indian host which the besieged whites estimated to be a full eight hundred strong. The hostiles were greatly encouraged by the presence of the heretofore invincible chief, and all were confident that the Forsyth expedition would be wiped out to the last man.

"Jee-hosaphat!" Henry Tucker exclaimed as he watched the Indians forming their ranks upstream. "This is gonna be one helluva charge!"

The Kansan nodded. "Looks like they mean business this time," he said gamely, turning to Soaring Hawk, who nodded back at him.

"They got ol' Roman Nose with 'em," Jack Poole observed.

"Who's he?" asked Dave.

"Craziest sum'bitch in these parts," Henry Tucker informed him. "They say bullets can't touch him."

"Well, now," Poole told his fellow-scout, hefting his "yellow boy" Winchester as he did, "I aim to disprove that. Right soon."

"You got your chance, Jack," Eli Zigler piped up. " 'Cause here they come!"

The Kansan leveled his Spencer and squinted along its barrel as Roman Nose led the Indians toward the island. Whooping and screaming like a legion of demons pouring forth out of the gates of hell, they made their way down the dry creek bed.

"Hold your fire until they are almost upon us!" Major Forsyth called out. "Make every shot count!"

"I couldn't agree more," Jack Poole muttered as he drew a bead on Roman Nose.

By the time they reached the upper end of the island, the hostiles were met by a withering hail of gunfire, one that was as telling as it was concentrated. The scouts were all crack shots, and they poured their fire into the ranks of the oncoming Cheyenne, Sioux and Arapaho warriors with deadly accuracy.

No sooner had his horse put hoof to the sand of Beecher's Island than the warchief pitched backwards out of his saddle, mortally wounded. A great cry of dismay went up from the ranks of the Indians as Roman Nose was dragged off.

"I got 'im! I got 'im!" Dave screamed ecstatically.

"The hell you did," Jack Poole informed him. "It was *my* shot what unhorsed him."

"Bull-dickey!" growled Henry Tucker. " 'Twas *my* bullet brought him down!"

"No, you're full of beans," corrected Jack Donovan. "I *am* the man who plugged ol' Roman Nose."

Soaring Hawk nudged the Kansan. "Now every man

here shoot Roman Nose." He shook his head. *"Just like white man."*

"Well, I hope to God you fellas will quit squabblin' soon," Eli Zigler told them between rifle shots, *"an help me out with them other eight hundred Injuns."*

The hostiles kept coming after Roman Nose had fallen, but the killing fire of the defenders was just too much for them. And when the charge had finally been broken, the Indians left scores of their dead upon the sands. Dry Arikaree Creek ran red with their blood.

. . .

All this transpired in an instant, the vivid memory triggered in the Kansan's brain by the sight of the Spencer rifles in the hands of the Indians who confronted him as he peered into the mouth of the cave. But as he came back to the present, Dave Watson was filled with the chilling awareness that his life and the life of Marcus Haverstraw depended upon the outcome of this surprise encounter.

The Kansan raised his eyes from the weapons to the faces of the Indians who held them. To his great surprise, Dave Watson saw that the braves were smiling at him! A moment later, after he had studied the braided hair of the Indians and the featherwork which adorned their persons, the Kansan smiled too.

Marcus Haverstraw gawked at his friend, as Dave Watson began to address the six braves before them, speaking in their own tongue, it appeared to the incredulous reporter. One of the Indians replied, causing Marcus' already wide eyes to go even wider, as he and the Kansan engaged in a conversation.

"It is good to see you again, Hammer Hand," the brave told Dave Watson, smiling fiercely as he did. He was a tall and wiry fellow with a prominent nose and dark, deep-set eyes. "Do you remember me?" he asked.

The Kansan nodded slowly, a smile of his own answering the Indian's. "How could I ever forget my brother, Red-Armed Panther?" he asked in turn. "How could I ever forget the man who went to shake my hand, and left me with the severed hand of a dead Cheyenne?"

All of the braves laughed at this, causing a startled Marcus Haverstraw to recoil, and take a step backward into the teeming rain that fell beyond the mouth of the cave. The storm was at its height now: peals of thunder rang loudly and echoed off the cliffs, and searing flashes of lightning illuminated the cave with their bleached and ghastly light.

"That was a good joke," the brave named Red-Armed Panther told Dave when he had stopped laughing. "What is my brother doing in this country?"

"My friend and I have come to hunt the Cheyenne,' was the Kansan's grim reply, and it was one which caused the braves to nod approvingly.

"Dave, who are these gentlemen?" Marcus asked out of the side of his mouth, as he came beside his trail mate.

"These boys is Pawnee," the Kansan told him with a smile. "They's my adopted people. I know 'em from way back. They's the same bunch that Soaring Hawk travels with."

"My God, but that's a bit of luck!" Marcus exclaimed in a voice colored by tones of relief.

"We, too, have been hunting Cheyenne," Red-Armed Panther informed Dave in Pawnee. "We have been scouting for the white chief, and now we have come home to our people for the winter."

The Kansan knew that the brave was referring to Frank North, a former clerk in a trading store who had demonstrated a high degree of military ability in 1864, when he recruited a number of Pawnees to serve in Major General Samuel Curtis' campaign against the Sioux and the Cheyennes. The Pawnees had notable success under North's astute leadership, repeating their victorious tactics once again in the Powder River campaign which General Patrick Connor led in the following year. And ever since those days, Frank North took to the field with from two to four companies of his now-famous Pawnee scouts. Under his leadership, the Pawnees had done well against their more powerful and fiercer hereditary enemies, the Cheyenne and the Sioux. The braves of the tribe displayed much enthusiasm for North, and the man himself had made a name in the West; he had risen from captain to major, and the ranks of his Pawnees had swelled from a band to a force that was presently almost as large as a battalion.

The Kansan was smiling broadly now, as he prepared to address the warrior who stood beaming at him with a crooked and wolfish smile. Not only had he been reunited with the Pawnees, his adopted people, but he had also come across the best Cheyenne-hunters in the world—Major Frank North's Pawnee scouts!

"And my brother, Soaring Hawk," Dave asked, pronouncing the name of the young Pawnee who was tied to him by the indissoluble bond of their common and mingled blood, "how is he?"

"He, too, has been with the great white chief for several moons," Red-Armed Panther told him. "He should be at the camp of our people when we return."

"Then I am coming with you," the Kansan told him quietly. "For I wish to see him again."

"That is good," said the brave, nodding as he turned to his fellows.

"That is good," the other Pawnees agreed. "Hammer Hand has come home."

Dave smiled at the name, which had been given to him by his blood-brother Soaring Hawk in admiration, after the latter had seen a barroom demonstration of the Kansan's devastating punch.

He stepped toward the braves, his arms held out at his sides, a smile upon his lips. And then he addressed the Pawnees in a hearty voice, one which carried over the detonations of thunder outside.

"I know you all," he told them as he came forward. "Red-Armed Panther. Wolf Voice. Long Knife. Bobtail Horse. Crazy Dog. Little Bear. I remember you all, my brothers." Saying this, he proceeded to shake hands with each of the Pawnees.

"Welcome, Hammer Hand," Long Knife told him. "Soaring Hawk will be very happy that his brother has returned."

"Running Buffalo will hold a feast in your honor," Wolf Voice said, mentioning the name of the chief of Soaring Hawk's tribe.

"And Plenty Bird will be glad, too," added Bobtail Horse, speaking the name of the chief's son.

"One other will be happy when Hammer Hand returns to the camp of our people," Red-Armed Panther said with a sly smile. The Kansan knew immediately who he meant, and his thoughts harked back to the young Pawnee beauty who had been his lover in the camp of Chief Running Buffalo. Her name was Bright Water, and she was the daughter of Dull Knife, brother to the chief.

"How is Bright Water?" he asked quietly, casting an involuntary glance at Marcus Haverstraw, even though the man understood not one word of the Pawnee tongue.

"She is well, my brother," Red-Armed Panther replied. "And her heart will be light when she sees Hammer Hand once more."

The other Pawnees all nodded at this, and grinned at the Kansan.

"What in the world are you discussing," Marcus said suddenly, "that could make you blush like that, David Lee?"

"Oh, uh . . . we's jus' talkin' over ol' times, me 'n the boys here," Dave mumbled, turning away from the journalist.

"This man is my friend," he told the braves, "a trail companion and a blood-brother to me among my people. He is a very wise man, one who knows many things about the world. He has been to many strange places, and has seen many of the different tribes and great cities of the white men."

"Is he a medicine man?" asked Red-Armed Panther, regarding Marcus Haverstraw with interest.

Dave grinned. "No, he is not."

"Is he a chief, then?" Wolf Voice asked.

"No, he is not a chief," the Kansan told him. "There is no word in the Pawnee language that I can think of to describe what my good friend does in the world."

The braves all exchanged puzzled looks.

"Does he have many possessions?" asked Bobtail

Horse. "Many horses?"

The Kansan shook his head.

"Does he have many wives?" Little Bear asked, followed by Crazy Dog, who asked, "And many strong and brave sons?"

"No, he has none of those," was Dave's reply to the Pawnees, who now looked perplexed in the extreme.

Little Bear held up his hands and said, "We do not understand what this man does in the world." Suddenly his face brightened. "He must be a good hunter. That is what he must be!"

The other braves all nodded their heads in agreement with this last statement.

The Kansan nodded his head. "He is a great hunter," he replied slowly. "But not in the way a Pawnee would expect. He is a great hunter of news—of the doings of men in the world, of the things which all people wish to know."

"Then he is a medicine man," Red-Armed Panther said with finality. "The spirits tell him these things. How could it be otherwise?"

Dave Watson sighed and pushed back his Stetson as he scratched his forehead, the look of perplexity that had been seen earlier upon the faces of the Pawnees now investing his own countenance. He had come to the limit of his ability to explain the newspaperman's profession to the Indians.

"What the devil were you boys wrangling about?" asked Marcus, who had observed the transaction with great interest.

"I, uh, was tryin' to explain to them boys what yer work was, but they took it to mean that you was some kind of medicine man."

"Ah, I see," the reporter murmured softly. "The problem is one of communication. These gentlemen are of a stage of civilization much simpler and earlier than our own mechanically-oriented state of existence. I imagine the difficulty lies in trying to explain the rather abstract concept that my work involves the collection and transmission of information. There is little of the concrete about it, except perhaps that I write on a pad with a pencil, and that I often use the marvelous invention of the telegraph to transmit said information."

"Yep, I reckon that's the problem," Dave Watson agreed. "Y'see, the Pawnees don't have no written language, an' I know fer a fact that most of 'em haven't caught hold of the idea behind the telegraph. It's like when the trains started to go across the plains, the Injuns used to think it was some sort of animal. Why, in the beginning, couple of years back, some of them bucks even tried to lassoo the damned steam engines."

"That's what it is, old man," Marcus said, "a problem in expression and conceptualization. I suppose you'd be wise to leave it at that, and let these gentlemen use the explanation which sits best with them."

"I reckon so," Dave agreed, turning back to the Indians and calling out each man's name as he formally introduced them to Marcus Haverstraw.

That done, the braves invited the two men to join them by the fire. Both Dave and Marcus did this willingly, for each was soaked to the skin by the torrential rains which continued to fall outside. Lightning still flashed on occasion, and thunder could still be heard, although its peals were now receding into the distance.

The Kansan and the reporter took off their wet clothing and wrapped themselves in the saddle blankets which the Pawnees offered them.

Soon the braves began to cook a small meal, to which the visitors added beans, hardtack and coffee. This last item, when sweetened by molasses, was much prized by the Indians of the Great Plains, and the six braves were delighted when the Kansan took the small coffee pout out of his saddle bag.

After the meal the men smoked, Indian-style, passing one pipe around as they talked of war and hunting and the senseless slaughter of the buffalo, which had noticeably begun to thin out the herds, although the great, shaggy beasts were still counted in the millions. The Pawnees, like all other Plains Indians, were greatly saddened and disturbed by the wanton slaughter of their sacred animal. The Kansan had no answer for them. He knew that what his people were doing was wrong and he was ashamed of it. At that moment, thinking of the corruption, crime, disease and exploitation the whites had brought to the Great Plains, Dave Watson was ashamed to claim such men as his own folks. Mercifully, this feeling did not last long, as the Indians and their white guests soon rolled themselves up in their blankets and went to sleep. There are few cases of insomnia on the trail. In the morning, they all began the journey back to the Pawnee camp, where Dave Watson would be reunited with his blood-brother, Soaring Hawk . . . and Bright Water.

After a journey which lasted almost two days, the riders finally reached the Pawnee camp. Marcus

Haverstraw was awed as he approached the spot where Dave Watson's adopted people had settled in for the winter. It was his first visit to such a place, and the reporter was thrilled, taking the exotic spectacle in with all the wonder and breathless excitement of a boy making his first visit to a county fair.

"So this is it, eh?" he murmured rapturously, leaning toward the Kansan, who rode beside him. "This is what it's really like?"

Dave grinned a him. "I reckon you'll find it a mite different from all that hogwash what ol' Ned Buntline done slopped out in his dime novels." He shook his head. "Why, that scoundrel ain't never been no nearer to an Injun camp than I been to a Zulu village in Africa."

"He, ah, was reputed to have served in the Seminole War, you know," Marcus informed him.

"Well, mebbe he done fought against the Seminoles," the Kansan conceded, "but he damn sure never spent any time amongst 'em. 'Less'n he was drunk at the time, an' forgot."

"From what Tim Fairwether told me," Marcus said, mentioning the name of a fellow reporter in New York City, "the odds are greatly in favor of that. The old curmudgeon has the nerve to deliver temperance lectures when he's had a snootful of booze."

"Well, this here's the real goods yer seein' now, ol' hoss. This is how yer Plains Injun lives."

The Kansan smiled as he said this, for as he looked upon the village a wave of memories broke inside his brain and immersed him in a flood of recollection.

His odyssey across the American continent had begun over three years ago, in the town of Hawkins Fort, in Anderson County, Kansas, where he had defended a young Indian brave who was being bullied in a barroom by a pack of desperadoes. That Indian was Soaring Hawk, who was destined to become blood-brother to the Kansan at the time, merely Davy Watson, a youngster who had not ranged far afield from his family's place on Pottawatomie Creek.

He had learned how to shoot before he left home, and the big, powerful youth could hold his own in a fight. Once on the trail, he learned the lessons of survival well from Soaring Hawk, and was an old hand three years later. But he was always open to learn something new. That was one of the Kansan's great strengths. Unlike many of his fellows who were gunfighters or lawmen or adventurers, Dave Watson was never too proud to reach out to others and ask for help. He came from pioneer stock, and regarded men and woman as equals, a fact he had seen demonstrated all his life, as his loving parents worked side by side on the Watson farm. That was the way of the early folk, although the lesson was most often lost on those who lived in towns and cities. But Dave Watson had a loving regard for women. They knew it, and trusted the Kansan in turn.

The whole business had started right after Dave met the woman he loved . . . in a Hawkins Fork bawdy house. And as he tried to defend Soaring Hawk against Ace Landry and his bully-boys in the Red Dog Saloon, the young Kansan was unexpectedly launched upon a career of adventure. As a result of this altercation, Dave and his beloved father, John Jacob Watson, were both shot down by Ace Landry.

The Kansan survived, but his father did not. In the

spring, when his wounds had healed, he set out on a quest for vengeance which took him across the North American continent. Adventure followed adventure, and complication followed complication; after he had achieved his ends, it took Dave Watson almost two and a half years to return to his home state. And when he did, it was to find that Deanna MacPartland had been kidnapped by John Hartung, a man who had a claim upon her loyalties.

In the course of his subsequent adventures, the Kansan had gone from St. Louis to New Orleans, where he took passage to the port of New York. But Hartung eluded him again, and he went west once more, in pursuit of Deanna's abductor. Back in the Sunflower state, where he had started out three years before, the Kansan discovered that Hartung had sold Deanna to Duncan Stearns, one of the most powerful men in the state. This precipitated a showdown at Stearns' saloon, wherein, aided by Marcus, Buffalo Bill Cody and Wild Bill Hickok, the Kansan discovered, after besting the huge and formidable Duncan Stearns, that Deanna was not on the premises.

She had been taken to Stearns' ranch, outside of Hays City. The Kansan and his party rode out there posthaste, but they were too late. The ranch had been burned to the ground by warring Indians, and Deanna MacPartland, Dave was later to learn, had been carried off by the Cheyenne warrior named Grey Thunder.

The Kansan had decided to get her back. If Grey Thunder was opposed to this, why, then he would have to fight for his life. *The issues were very simple: Life and Death. That was all.*

Nothing had changed, it seemed as the Kansan rode

121

up to the Pawnee camp; and he experienced a sudden feeling of timelessness as he viewed the Indian encampment. All Indian camps looked much the same each time one returned to them, Dave realized; but he felt as if he were coming to visit Soaring Hawk's people for the very first time. And yet, at the same moment in which he experienced this feeling, the Kansan was also glad to be returning. It felt, he realized with wonder, as if he were about to visit close relatives or friends after a long absence. It was good to be coming home. These were his adopted people.

Smoke arose from the cooking fires and drifted up to the clear blue sky in lazy, wavering swirls. As the riders approached the camp, whose teepee gleamed softly with the light of the winter's day, the ever-present dogs trotted to the perimeter of the settlement and observed the newcomers, sniffing the air. And then, when they were satisfied with the results of their olfactory intelligence, the animals ran out to greet the visitors.

"Hammer Hand!" men and woman told each other as the Kansan rode in alongside the warriors. *"Hammer Hand has returned! Hammer Hand is back!"*

The Kansan grinned as he heard this, and nodded his head as he looked around, recognizing a familiar face at every turn. There was Dull Knife. And Big Ox. Running Deer, cousin of Bright Water, and daughter of the chief. Dirty Nose, the little boy who had always followed him around the camp like a shadow. And old Wailing Woman. And Black Crow. And Big Heart. So many old friends! He felt as if he were attending a family reunion. And then the Kansan caught sight of Soaring Hawk. . . .

He looked deep into his Pawnee blood-brother's

dark eyes, smiling immediately with recognition. It was the same old Soaring Hawk. The same broad-cheekboned face and prominent nose, the same gleaming smile and lustrous black hair. The same proud bearing and wise, penetrating glance. The same catlike movements and easy, animal grace, a little older and wiser-looking, perhaps, but essentially the same Soaring Hawk whom he remembered, the same man who had ridden beside him in many adventures.

The Kansan rode over to where Soaring Hawk was standing. As he did, the brave asked in the Pawnee tongue, "What brings my brother back to the camp of Running Buffalo?"

"I have come here because I am hunting," was Dave Watson's terse reply.

"And what does Hammer Hand hunt?" the Pawnee asked.

"Cheyenne," the Kansan told him, his eyes flashing as he said the word.

Soaring Hawk laughed. "That is fit sport for a Pawnee. Maybe we will help you."

"It is my hope that you do."

"What Cheyenne do you seek, my brother?"

"I seek a warrior named Grey Thunder. He has taken Deanna, and I intend to kill him."

The young brave nodded, his face expressionless. "Then I will surely help you take this man's scalp. The Cheyenne are no friends of the Pawnee. I will help you, Hammer Hand. And if you tell your story before Running Buffalo and the elders of the tribe, perhaps others will help you as well."

The Kansan smiled at the young Pawnee. "My brother gladdens my heart. If ever there was a time that

I needed his help, that time is now."

"I hear you, my brother," Soaring Hawk told him, as Dave leaned forward in the saddle and shook his hand.

"We will find your woman, Hammer Hand," Soaring Hawk promised his blood-brother. Then he grinned fiercely. "And we will take many Cheyenne scalps."

"I know one I'm gon' git me, fer sure," Dave muttered. Then he turned and indicated Marcus Haverstraw with a wave of his hand. The reporter sat on his horse some ten feet behind the Kansan.

"Remember this fella?" he asked Soaring Hawk in English.

The Pawnee nodded. "This is man who help us in Virginia City and big settlement of the white men by the water," he answered, referring to San Francisco, where he, Dave and Marcus had come to rescue the three Mundree sisters, those Boise girls who had been kidnapped and sold into white slavery.

"How do you do, Mister Hawk," the newspaperman said, beaming at the brave.

Soaring Hawk grinned at Marcus. "You come to take Cheyenne scalp?"

Marcus winced at this, and cleared his throat before he replied. "I, ah, came to help Dave get Deanna Mac-Partland back. But when you ride with this fellow, you usually get more than you bargained for. That much I know. But in answer to your question, Mister Hawk, no, it is not my custom to take scalps."

Both Soaring Hawk and the Kansan grinned at him.

"I, ah, have been known to fire the occasional shot in self defense," Marcus went on, flushing as he perceived that his listeners were amused by his words.

"But I do not deem it necessary to go so far as to lift the scalp of a fallen enemy." He raised his hands in the air. "and actually, gentlemen, I have not yet lost all hope of a peaceful settlement."

Soaring Hawk frowned at this. "Not with Cheyenne," he told the reporter, a tone of grim finality in his voice. "Cheyenne fight to death. To get Hammer Hand's woman back from Grey Thunder, you must kill him." Here the Pawnee flashed Marcus a wicked smile as he fingered the razor-sharp scalping knife at his belt, the very knife, Marcus recollected with sudden queasiness, that he had used to gut an attacker in San Francisco. "And kill him is what we must do. And when that is done . . . I will lift Grey Thunder's scalp."

Marcus sighed as he realized that he was once more about to become embroiled in a life-and-death adventure with the Kansan.

"Jus' think of the great story yer gon' have when all the shootin's over, Marcus," Dave Watson told him.

The reporter heaved a second heavy sigh. "Yes, I know, old chap. And I fervently hope that I shall be around to write said story after the shooting's all over."

"You been mightly lucky so far," the Kansan reminded him, grinning at Soaring Hawk. "Y'know, me'n Marcus been in a lot of scrapes since we last seen each other, my brother," he told the brave. "An ol' Marcus may be a peaceable fella, but he shore can take care of himself when push comes to shove."

"Shove," said his Pawnee blood-brother loudly. "That was the name of big fat man you shoot down in Virginia City."

"Yep. That's right, ol' hoss," Dave Watson told him, grinning wryly as he recalled his pistol duel on Mount

Davidson with the corpulent and deadly Alabama procurer. He had lost an earlobe in that contest, and as the Kansan recollected the details of the encounter, he absent-mindedly fingered the scar of the wound.

"Ah, yes, Malcolm Shove," said Marcus Haverstraw, himself having been one of Dave's seconds. "And he was the odds'on favorite to win."

"Ya never know, do ya?" murmured the Kansan.

"I guess not," was the newspaperman's whispered reply.

"Now we together again," Soaring Hawk said. "We have good times." He turned and motioned for Dave and Marcus to follow him. "Tonight there will be big feast in your honor."

You see, I am alive.
You see, I stand in good relation to the earth.
You see, I stand in good relation to the gods.
You see, I stand in good relation to all that is
  beautiful.
You see, I stand in good relation to you.
You see, I am alive. I am alive.

The Kansan remembered the words of an ancient Indian chant, the one which his blood-brother had chanted to him on the night before he last rode out of the camp of his adopted people. That was in the days which had followed the arduous crossing of the Southwest which he and Soaring Hawk had made after they left San Francisco and had parted company with Marcus Haverstraw.

He remembered those days, as well: days of love and

violence among the *chicanos* and Anglos of the New Mexico Territory, and the fierce Apaches of Arizona. The Kansan gritted his teeth as he remembered, with sudden and painful clarity, the fifty lashes which had been administered to him at Fort Burnside on the order of Major Jock Forbes. And then he remembered the deadly ambush in which the Chiricahua Apaches, led by none other than the redoubtable Cochise, had annihilated a troop of United States Cavalry after Soaring Hawk had freed the notorious warchief Geronimo from the Phoenix jailhouse.

There had been much violence and pain beneath the red Apache sun of the southwest; but there had been other things, as well. Dave remembered Consuela Delgado, the dark-eyed, loving *Mexicana* who had befriended him at the house of Darrell Duppa, the Englishman who had given Phoenix its name. And he remembered Raquel Mirabel, the lovely young *chicana,* the daughter of a New Mexican *rico,* the woman whom he had made love to on horseback, after the fashion of the Comanches and the Russian Cossacks. And then the Kansan's smile hardened and froze into a tight, grim line, as he suddenly remembered the enemies of those hard days.

Paul Hutzelman, the bounty hunter known as *Killer-of-Apaches* by the Chiricahua themselves, the captor of both Geronimo and the Kansan Captain Daniel Patrick Haggerty, the corpulent Irish killer whose infamous gang of desperadoes known as Haggerty's Hellions terrorized West Texas from El Paso to Laredo; Bart Braden, the toughest, hardest and most resourceful man that Dave Watson had ever met, the man who had gunned him down and almost killed him. . . .

He and Soaring Hawk had come a long way together, the Kansan reminded himself as he returned to the present. And now they were reunited, and the circle was unbroken: Soaring Hawk had ridden out with him at the beginning of his odyssey over three years ago, and now he would ride beside him as it came to its end. The Kansan smiled at this thought. He knew that he would get Deanna back from Grey Thunder or die in the attempt.

Despite this grim thought, he was smiling as he entered the great teepee of Running Buffalo, chief of Soaring Hawk's people. Dave Watson's heart was light as he looked around the circle of the hide-covered tent and recognized so many familiar faces.

Plenty Bird, the chief's son was there, as was his uncle, Dull Knife. He also recognized several of the Pawnee scouts he had encountered on the trail two days ago, Red-Armed Panther and Bobtail Horse. The faces of the elders were familiar to him, as well. Only one face from the past was missing, the medicine man, White Wolf.

The chief, looking much the same as Dave remembered him, with long, grey-shot braids, furrowed and leathery face, and great, wise eyes, motioned across the fire for the Kansan to come and sit at his right hand. This Dave Watson did with alacrity, and murmured in the Pawnee speech as he sat down.

"It is good to be back in the camp of Running Buffalo," the Kansan told the grizzled old chief. "And it is good to be among so many good friends and brave men."

The Indians, who all sat in the customary circle whose center was the small fire which burnt in the teepee, murmured their approval of this sentiment and nodded greetings at Dave Watson.

"It is good to have our brother Hammer Hand back in the tents of the Pawnee," old Running Buffalo said after lighting a long pipe and taking several puffs on it.

"I thank the chief for his eternal kindness and hospitality," the Kansan replied, taking the pipe which Running Buffalo had proffered.

"Soaring Hawk tells me that Hammer Hand is hunting Cheyennes," the old Indian said, nodding at Dave's blood-brother, who sat at his left hand, just beyond his son, Plenty Bird.

This remark elicited many grins and knowing, hungry looks from the assembled Pawnees, who were the hereditary enemies of the Cheyenne.

Dave nodded his head as he puffed on the pipe. And then, as he exhaled a mouthful of smoke and passed the pipe to the old Pawnee on his right, he said, "That is true, O Running Buffalo. A Cheyenne warrior named Grey Thunder has stolen my woman, and I intend to kill him and take her back with me."

Grey Thunder was obviously known to the assemblage, and the Kansan heard his name mentioned several times as the Pawnees muttered among themselves.

"Soaring Hawk also tells me that he wishes to accompany his brother on the great hunt," the old chief said, once the Pawnees had quieted down.

Dave looked at Soaring Hawk, who locked eyes with him and nodded his head slowly and emphatically.

"I would welcome my brother's aid," the Kansan told Chief Running Buffalo.

The old Indian nodded, his facial expression severe. "Many of my young braves have asked permission to accompany you on this hunt, my son. They have come to me, saying 'The Cheyenne are our enemies, as well as those of our brother, Hammer Hand. Let us go with him, O Chief. Let us come to the assistance of Soaring Hawk's blood-brother.'"

The old man looked deep into the Kansan's eyes. "And I have said to the braves, 'Hammer Hand is one of us. He is a Pawnee. You may ride with him when he goes to kill Grey Thunder and bring his woman back. So be it.'"

Dave placed an arm across his chest, closed fist resting upon his heart. "Thank you, Father," he told Running Buffalo. "I am most grateful to you and my brothers for your aid in my time of need."

Understanding none of this exchange, which had been conducted in Pawnee, Marcus Haverstraw looked on with interest nevertheless, his newspaperman's instincts telling him that something of great importance was transpiring before his eyes. And so, as he puffed on the long clay pipe filled with tobacco that had been combined with dogwood bark and buffalo dung, he carefully studied the faces and listened to the voices of Dave Watson and the Pawnee chief.

"Grey Thunder travels with a band of twenty or so warriors, some of the Sioux and Arapaho," the Kansan told his listeners. "Or at least he did before the winter came."

Running Buffalo nodded. "The Sioux and Arapaho have probably returned to their own people, unless they, too, are outlaws. We know that Grey Thunder has been banished from his tribe."

It was the Kansan's turn to nod. "What does Running Buffalo judge to be the best time to resume the

Cheyenne hunt?" he asked.

"It will be very difficult to locate Grey Thunder's winter camp," the old man told him. "But with the coming of spring he will be out upon the plains again. And like the other people of the plains, he and his warriors will go to hunt the buffalo. It is then you will find him, my son.' He shook his head. "Not before."

Dave nodded respectfully to the chief, and then turned to Marcus Haverstraw. "I hope you ain't in no all-fired hurry to git back to New Orleans and yer lady," he said. " 'Cause the chief jus' advised me to cool my heels 'til spring."

Marcus looked relieved. "Frankly, I have no objection whatever to that sage bit of advice, old man." He sighed and shot the Kansan a sheepish look. "Actually, I was, ah, rather hoping that we'd get a chance to put in somewhere." The reporter shivered. I wasn't at all looking forward to getting trapped in a blizzard while on the trail, you know."

Dave Watson nodded tiredly. "Can't say as I blame ya, ol' hoss. You got yerself a point, there."

"I'm glad that you see it that way."

"You ever spend the winter in an Injun camp?" a grinning Kansan asked Marcus.

"No," he replied. "But I'm certainly willing to do so at present." He grinned back at Dave. "I imagine that it should be quite an extraordinary experience."

"Oh, it's somethin' to write home about, all right," Dave Watson agreed. "Ain't you comin' to miss ol' Della a bit these days, Marcus?" the Kansan asked, referring to the black New Orleans courtesan who had become the newspaperman's lover.

"More than you could imagine," was the latter's

glum reply. "But I'm determined to see this story through to the end. I don't do things by halfway measures."

"No, you don't ol' hoss. That's fer sure," Dave said admiringly. "You hang on like some damn bulldog. I got to hand it to ya, Marcus. You sure ain't in no way short on spunk."

The pipe came back to Running Buffalo. "Now we will smoke to the success of the great Cheyenne hunt," he said solemnly, holding the pipe up in the air with both hands and thrusting it toward each of the four points of the compass. "May all those who have joined Hammer Hand have good medicine. And may our brother have good medicine."

The mention of medicine brought the Kansan's thoughts racing back to the one familiar face that had been missing from the conclave in Running Buffalo's teepee. Where was White Wolf? he asked himself. Where was the Pawnee medicine man who had foreseen his long odyssey across the North American continent? Where was the old Indian shaman who had known that he had much to endure before his long, hard ride would end?

"Father," he said to the chief, "where is White Wolf?"

Running Buffalo finished puffing on the pipe, and then handed it to the Kansan. "Death took him, my son. Two moons ago," was his reply.

Dave nodded his head. "That man had big medicine, O Chief. He foretold my future."

"He was a great medicine man," the chief agreed. "But Death took him, all the same."

Dave nodded again, knowing that the issue was

132

closed. But he felt an eerie chill as he recollected the strange old medicine man's behavior on his last visit to the Pawnee camp. White Wolf had somehow known that his trail was not yet to be ended, that he had more hardship to endure. He would have been more reassured had the old man been present at the teepee, Dave felt, but at the same time he was relieved by the fact that the grim old prophet would no longer be able to scowl at him from across the fire in Running Buffalo's tent.

The future would take care of itself, the Kansan thought. It was far, far better not to know what it held in store. He would be content to take all the actions of which he was capable; and then, he would pray and hope for the best. There was no more that he could do. Dave Watson believed that he could only live one day at a time. Yesterday was past, and tomorrow had not yet arrived; today was all that he had. It was enough for him. He would attend to tomorrow when it became today.

After the discussion in the chief's teepee, the Pawnees reached deep into their meager winter stores and prepared a feast in honor of Hammer Hand's return. Jerked beef, cornmeal cakes, dried venison and buffalo meat, roots and seeds, and a stew whose meat, the Kansan informed a wide-eyed Marcus, was one or two of the dogs who had greeted them as they rode into the camp.

After the meal there was singing and dancing, all of which the insatiably curious Marcus Haverstraw watched with great pleasure. The men danced hunting dances and war dances, and the young, unmarried women of the tribe danced as well.

"Look at that tall young beauty, David Lee!" the reporter exclaimed. "My God, but she's striking!"

The Kansan nodded and shot him a knowing look. "That there's Bright Water," he told the newspaperman in a low voice, a voice had had a discernible ring of pride to it.

"Ah," Marcus whispered, his face lighting up, "so *that's* the celebrated Pawnee belle! She certainly is a most attractive young woman." He looked toward the tall, lissome beauty, just as she wheeled and turned not more than ten feet from where they sat in the huge ceremonial teepee of Chief Running Buffalo. "And I can see that she's still got eyes for you, old man."

"We, uh, go back a ways together," the Kansan muttered, suddenly flushing in the firelight.

"She seems to remember that fact, too," the newspaperman said gaily. "I don't think you're going to have to spend such a cold winter, after all."

Dave Watson flushed again and turned back to watch the young women of the Pawnee tribe dance. But when he looked up at Bright Water again, the tall, dark-haired young squaw's eyes met his.

Damn! he said to himself. *That gal gits more beautiful each time I come back here. And she moves like a mountain lion on the prowl. Why, she's glidin' light as a spring wind on the open range. Wonder if she still likes to go off by herself an' stare up at the moon an' stars? Wonder if she got her eye on any of these fine young fellas hereabouts? I wonder jus' how that sweet ol' gal is, anyway?*

He was soon to know; for after the celebration,

when the tribe had all gone to sleep, Soaring Hawk came into the teepee which he now shared with Dave and Marcus, leading a figure wrapped in a blanket.

"Old friend come visit you, Hammer Hand," he told the Kansan in English. Then he turned to journalist, who was sitting down on a blanket, about to take his boots off.

"Marcus," the brave whispered. "Red-Armed Panther and Little Bear tell me they heap proud to have you visit their tent, and sleep there tonight. You come now, I take you there."

"Ah, yes," Marcus grunted as he staggered to his feet. "Of course, Mister Hawk. I would consider it a great privilege to be the guest of such esteemed gentlemen. Please lead the way."

"Thanks, Marcus," the Kansan murmured as the newspaperman passed by him.

"That's what friends are for, m'boy," Marcus Haverstraw told him, ducking down to pass through the opening of the teepee.

"Good night, Hammer Hand," Soaring Hawk whispered in parting.

"Good night, my brother," the Kansan whispered back, now alone in the teepee with the tall, blanket-shrouded figure.

"Who comes to see me when all the people of Running Buffalo are asleep?" he asked in Pawnee, his voice a whisper.

"One who is an even bigger fool than you," a woman's voice replied as the Indian blanket fell to the ground.

6

DUNCAN STEARNS RALLIES HIS FORCES

"Come over here and sit by me," the Kansan said in a husky voice as he looked into the night-dark eyes of Bright Water, daughter of Dull Knife and niece to Running Buffalo.

Slowly, seductively, her eyes never leaving the Kansan's face, the tall young Pawnee came toward him with a dancer's grace. The hanging strips of her buckskin skirt rustled softly and the beads around her long, slim neck chukked in a minor key, the only sounds in the tent other than the occasional crackling and popping of the fire's embers. Her step was so light that the Kansan could not hear it, even though he strained his ears. And it was in silence that the lissome young beauty sat down beside him on his blanket.

Bright Water said nothing as she sat beside the Kansan, but her eyes spoke volumes. Dave saw the deep longing in them, the hunger and the desire. And when she saw that he was studying her, she lowered her head.

"When I last rode out from the camp of Running Buffalo, Bright Water was still a girl. Now she has become a woman, with all a woman's beauty. It is good to see the daughter of Dull Knife once more," the Kansan said.

"Hammer Hand looks older, too," she said with a trace of sarcasm.

The Kansan grinned at her. "He is very tired, and has been on the trail for too many moons. He yearns to rest and settle down."

"Is Hammer Hand not married yet?" she asked, her eyes upon the ground.

Dave sighed heavily when he heard this. "Not yet," he said quietly.

"I have heard that your woman has been taken by a Cheyenne warrior," Bright Water said. "Is this true?"

The Kansan nodded. "I have come out on the plains to find her . . . and kill him. My Pawnee brothers have decided to ride out with me when the spring comes. And then I shall settle the score with this man."

Her expression changed upon hearing these last words. "Then you will stay here until the spring comes?" she asked in a small, hopeful voice.

"That is true," Dave Watson told Bright Water. "I will stay with Running Buffalo and his people until the winter has passed."

"That is good," she murmured, blushing.

The Kansan reached out his hand and lifted her head, gazing deep into Bright Water's dark and gleaming eyes. "It is good to see my old friend again," he told her in a husky voice.

Slowly her eyes traveled up over Dave's chest, neck and face. "It is good to see Hammer Hand," she told him in turn, her voice barely audible.

"Will you stay with me tonight?" he asked her.

137

Bright Water nodded. "You know that. And any other night you wish."

He took his hand from beneath her chin and caressed her cheek. "It is good to see Bright Water. My heart is full now. I have had a very lonely time. I have been cold and hungry for a long time. But now I am warm once more."

The young woman nodded, too overcome with the emotion she felt to be able to reply.

"And Dull Knife's daughter surpasses all the women of the Pawnee in grace and beauty," Dave went on. "She must have many suitors. Many young braves must come to the tent of her father."

Bright Water blushed again.

"Many horses must be offered for her," the Kansan went on, grinning at her discomfiture. "Many swift ponies must have been promised to Dull Knife in return for his beautiful daughter."

"It is true," she whispered, her voice barely audible above the crackling of the fire. "Many men have asked my father to give me to them. But he is kind to his daughter. He says he will wait until I tell him which man among the Pawnees it is to be."

"And does Bright Water know this yet?" Dave Watson asked.

She sighed. "There is one man that Bright Water holds in her heart . . . but he has not promised her father any ponies. And he has a woman already." She raised her eyes and gave him a meaningful look.

"That is how it is," he murmured, his smile going sad. "I have been pledged to this woman for more than three years, as you well know. Since the days before we met. And now she has been stolen from me, and I intend to get her back."

"And then what?" she asked, suddenly lowering her eyes before the Kansan could reply.

"When I get her back," he said simply, "I will marry her. And we will live on my place by Pottawatomie Creek."

Bright Water gave a small gasp as he said this. The Kansan shook his head and took her hand.

"That is how it must be, my friend." he said tenderly, squeezing her hand. "That is how the spirits meant it to be."

Bright Water did not reply to this. A look of dejection overspread her features.

The Kansan squeezed her hand again. "There is no reason for Dull Knife's daughter to be sad, for she may have her pick among all the bravest warriors of the Pawnee in Running Buffalo's camp. Of all the camps of the Pawnee, I am certain!"

Still the young squaw said nothing, nor raised her eyes to meet the Kansan's inquiring glance.

"Soon she will find a man who pleases her," he went on, squeezing her hand a third time. "Soon Bright Water will find a warrior who moves her heart and fills it with pride."

"I already have," she murmured shyly, raising her eyes and looking into his. "He is with me now."

The Kansan cleared his throat. "And this man has much feeling for Bright Water. You know that."

She lowered her eyes at this and slowly nodded her head.

"But our paths are different, even though they have crossed several times." He squeezed her hand once again and she looked up, into the Kansan's clear blue eyes.

"And my heart is always moved by my sister, Bright Water. I believe she knows that very well."

"She knows that," the young beauty whispered in a husky voice, her look comingling love, sadness, hope and resignation. "But her heart has been given to Hammer Hand."

Dave took her in his arms and drew her to him slowly. "Then she must take it back, and give it to another," he whispered, feeling her body tremble as he held it against his. "For that is the way of life. Bright Water must do this once I am gone from here."

"But not until then," she whispered huskily, just before they kissed.

The Kansan took her down on the blanket, his tongue entering Bright Water's mouth and encountering hers in the process. She hugged him to her with surprising strength, and shuddred violently, breathing heavily all the time. And then, as the Kansan heard her moan, her lips still pressed firmly to his, he realized with a start that Bright Water was having an orgasm.

"Judas Priest, you're hotter than a pistol, gal," he murmured in English when their lips parted.

"I have missed you very much," she said, hugging him as she lay her head back down upon the blanket. "And now, this is to be the last season of my love for you. You, the man who awakened all these strong feelings within, feelings which sweep over me like the wind that sweeps down over the open plains."

"We have some time together, my sister," he whispered as they sat up on the blanket once more. And then he helped Bright Water out of her beaded shawl and buckskins. The Kansan stood up and began to take off his clothes, turning to the fire and feeling the young Pawnee's eyes upon his as he did.

She was naked and ardent and open-armed as he knelt down beside her upon the blanket. The tent was chilly, and so the Kansan had thrown some wood upon the fire, causing it to flare up brightly for several moments and impart its reddish glow to Bright Water's copper skin.

They embraced once more and caressed, hugging and kissing hungrily. The Kansan ran his hands along her trim flanks and over her pert, tight buttocks. And then she sighed like the wind in autumn as his hands snaked along the smooth, silky insides of her thighs. And when he cupped her black-thatched pussy and entered it with his middle finger, causing Bright Water to moan and gasp, Dave found that it was wet with the juices of her arousal.

He gently inserted another finger inside her, and then another. And then, as he began to work them in and out of her distended vagina, Bright Water squirmed and moaned like a cat in heat. Her thighs quivered as she shuddered in response to his touch, and the Kansan watched as she threw back her head and shut her eyes.

"Ooooooh," she gasped, arching her pelvis as he continued to probe and stroke her. *"Oooooooooh,"* And then, just as her whole form quivered, she cried out softly like a bird of the forest, repeating that cry with open mouth and closed eyes until she sank back onto the blanket, her climax attained.

The Kansan slid his fingers out of Bright Water's honeypot, catching the scent of a musky perfume as he did. "Bright Water is certainly glad to see me," he told her, grinning down at the spent and shaken young woman.

"When you look at me," she told him several moments later, breathing heavily as she did, "a fire starts inside me. A fire that sweeps over me like fire over the prairie."

"You was sure burnin' this time," he murmured, stroking the side of her high-cheekboned face.

"Will this happen again . . . when you are gone from my side?" Bright Water asked Dave Watson. "When you are gone from me forever? Will it happen . . . with another man?"

The Kansan flushed and turned away from her searching eyes, toward the crackling fire. He was silent for a long time, as he thought of an answer to her question.

"It will happen," he told her haltingly, a solemn expression upon his handsome, square-jawed face, "whenever Bright Water makes love with a man she loves and trusts. Whenever she gives herself to a man she cares for—a man who truly cares for her."

He turned back to Bright Water, his eyes now meeting hers. "For that is the secret of making the best love: The heart must speak, and be moved. You must have feeling for your lover." He shook his head slowly. "Otherwise, it is no different than what the camp dogs do when they couple."

"You truly think that I will find some man to fill my heart the way Hammer Hand does?" Bright Water asked the Kansan, reaching out a hand and running her fingers through the matted hair on his broad chest.

"If you choose well," he replied softly, lightly running his fingers over her lips. "If you truly listen to your heart."

"That is one reason I am drawn to you," she told him, tugging lightly at the hairs of his chest for emphasis. "You think like an Indian, and not like a white man."

His eyes widened at this. "What is the difference?"

She smiled at him. "A white man thinks with this," Bright Water told him, pointing to her head. "But an Indian thinks with this." Here she pointed to her heart.

He returned her smile, although his had a trace of sadness in it. "That is true enough, in a way," Dave replied. "Too many of my white brothers do not listen to their hearts. That is the tragedy of my people."

"They do not live in the world," Bright Water said. "They are always dissatisfied with things as they are. And they must always change things."

"Many of them are like that," Dave whispered back. "But not all." He smiled as he thought of the Watson farm on Pottawatomie Creek. "My father loved the land as much as any Indian loves the open plains. The wind sang to him like a woman. And the wheat danced for him in the wind, like the daughters of the Pawnee. Not all white men are like those who have destroyed the land and slaughtered the buffalo."

"Not all perhaps," she conceded. "But far too many."

"You are right there," he agreed. "But all that is far from us tonight . . . and we are here together."

"Yes, we are," she murmured, stroking his broad back.

"And I will take pleasure in your company." She kissed his back lightly several times. "And now, I will give my warrior pleasure," Bright Water whispered, darting her tongue in his ear. "Lie down."

He did, and she hovered over him, kissing his face and stroking his chest. It was the Kansan's turn to close his eyes, and he lay back upon the blanket and groaned like a bull in heat as the Indian beauty kissed and caressed her way along his body.

Her hands fluttered like mating turtle doves, their fingers igniting his passion with wingtip softness. Her mouth and tongue were on his chest now, and headed for his belly, reminding him of butterflies grazing among the spring flowers. Goose bumps rose up on his flesh, causing Dave to shiver with delight and the expectation of things to come. Indian women, he knew, were not usually as forward as Bright Water, and he was surprised by this. But he attributed this change in the young Pawnee's demeanor to the fact that this would be their last season together, and when he rode out of the camp of Running Buffalo this time, they would no longer be lovers. He knew that she understood that, and he was pleased to discover that she was acting like an Indian in this matter as well, living totally in the present. She was immersed in the fast-flowing tide of her love and passion, and Bright Water was determined to sweep the Kansan away in its strong currents.

Her tongue was circling his navel now, and her hands stroked his flanks and the insides of his thighs. A slow, warm glow began to build in the pit of his groin, and Dave Watson emitted another low groan. That groan turned to a short gasp as Bright Water's cool fingers closed around the shaft of his sex. And then his eyes opened involuntarily as the Kansan felt her lips brush his penis.

Snorting though his nose, Dave closed his eyes once more and surrendered to the surging heat which now infused his shuddering loins. He hissed through clenched teeth as the young Pawnee beauty took him into her mouth. And then he moaned as her darting tongue began a series of prolonged and intricate oral caresses.

She held his rod with one hand as she worked her mouth on its head, stroking it at the same time. The Kansan's body began to stiffen and she could hear him hiss like a rattlesnake that had just been flushed from a gully. His fingers dug into the blanket and then his hands clenched convulsively. Feeling this, Bright Water applied herself even more diligently, her tongue circling with salamandrine rapidity and her wet, warm mouth sucking, stroking and cupping all at the same time.

"Who-o-o-oa!" the Kansan grunted, his eyes rolling up in his head and his toes curling. *"Oh-h-h-hhhh, Ju-u-u-das Priest!"* he moaned as his pelvis began to twitch.

Lick. Suck. Stroke. Bright Water redoubled her efforts, knowing that the Kansan was about to climax. With feverish intensity the Pawnee beauty applied her hand and mouth to the Kansan's sex, her motions accompanied by his labored breathing.

"Ooo-who-o-o-oph-h-h-hhh!" grunted Dave Watson, eyes closed and mouth wide open as his jissum shot forth with all the force of water bursting an earthen dam. He bucked and twitched and groaned and snorted until the massive spasm had passed, and then, with a sigh not unlike the sound made by an expiring bull buffalo, the Kansan was still.

"I am glad you have come back," Bright Water whispered in Dave Watson's ear, snuggling up beside him on the Indian blanket. "Even if it is for the last time." She leaned over and regarded him in silence for a long time.

"What is Bright Water thinking?" the Kansan asked finally, breaking the heavy stillness that pervaded the teepee.

"I am thinking," she whispered, "that I must play out the last of my love in this cold season. I am thinking that I shall give you as much of myself as I can . . . and then let you go." She began to stroke his brow. "For I know how dangerous your quest will be. I must get used to the idea that I shall never see you again—at least the way you are to me at this moment."

He reached up a hand and gently ran his fingers over her temple and cheek. And as he did, Dave felt the wetness of he young Pawnee's tears.

"Either you will be married when all is said and done," Bright Water continued, her voice suddenly husky, "or you will be dead."

The snow continued to fall in the upper reaches of the Platte River, where Grey Thunder had his camp, and with it fell the spirits of Deanna MacPartland. The little blonde had begun to despair of ever being reunited with Dave Watson.

The last time she had seen the Kansan was on the easternmost tip of Long Island, as he lay crippled and helpless upon the sandy earth of the South Country Road, when John Hartung had carried her off in his rig. She didn't even know where he was today.

A tear trickled down her cheek. She had waited so long for Dave to return, and now things were much less hopeful than they had been at the beginning of her lover's long and perilous quest, when he and Soaring Hawk rode out after Ace Landry and his gang of desperadoes, seeking revenge for the death of the Kansan's father. Now, she told herself, he was crippled, or worse; and she was the captive of the fierce Cheyenne warrior, Grey Thunder.

It seemed so long ago, Deanna realized with a sigh as she drew her buffalo robe closer around her slender body and stared into the embers of the fire in Grey Thunder's tent. She had been full of so many hopes in those days, despite her fears that one day Dave Watson's mother would come to learn that the young woman her son intended to marry had worked as a brothel girl. And indeed, Deanna remained at the bawdy house of Mrs. Lucretia Eaton when the Kansan had ridden out of the town of Hawkins Fork. He had promised to return, at which time he would negotiate with the procuress for Deanna's release. But before Dave had completed that long trail of vengeance and adventure, John Hartung, the man who had saved her life years before and taken her to the establishment of Lucretia Eaton, had abducted her, intending to sell her to a procurer in New Orleans in order to pay off his gambling debts.

The little blonde sighed as she turned over, her face now toward the skins that covered the tent. John Hartung had no further claim upon her, she told herself; death had cleared the books. And although he had done her and the Kansan grievous harm, she did not look upon the man as evil.

He was sick, she told herself. His gambling had become an addiction, a vice which consumed everything else in his life. John Hartung, who had presumed to sell Deanna MacPartland, had himself been a slave, the prisoner of his addiction to gambling. He had been imprisoned within his vice just as surely as if he had been a drunkard or a glutton or a dope fiend. But now he was dead. Deanna winced at the memory of Hartung's scalp being lifted by Grey Thunder. *Rest in peace, John Hartung. May the Lord have mercy upon your soul.*

Just then she heard Grey Thunder call her name. Biting her lip, Deanna turned slowly and cocked an eye at the brave who lay beside her in the teepee. He shifted and smacked his lips, and then was still. The Cheyenne had not awakened; he had called out her name in his sleep, from within the remote land of his dreams.

Deanna studied Grey Thunder's face for a long while, the dying firelight playing over her delicate features. He was a virile and powerful man, in many ways an extraordinary specimen. He had sworn war to the death upon the whites, and now fought them at every turn. Grey Thunder was a natural leader and a shrewd tactician; Deanna was becoming aware of that as she learned more of the Cheyenne language each day. He was a man, she grudgingly admitted, who had few peers.

He certainly seemed to have a weakness for her, Deanna reminded herself as her eyes traveled over the Cheyenne's ruggedly handsome face and down to his naked chest. Perhaps that would turn out to be this otherwise invincible warrior's Achilles' heel. One never knew. It appeared that Grey Thunder was so taken with his "golden woman" that he even called for her in his sleep.

This naturally aroused the jealousy of the Cheyenne

women, who were as a rule a very independent and sharp-tongued lot. But none of them had said anything to Deanna, for fear of a beating by Grey Thunder, whose word was law in the little camp. She could sense it all the same, and knew that she was resented, even though the Cheyenne warriors occasionally took captive women as their wives. But Grey Thunder was the son of Flying Eagle, the peace chief of his particular Cheyenne band, and it was possible, she had come to learn, that when his exile was over and he had sworn nevermore to deviate from the Cheyenne way, that he might then become the war chief of his people. There was no doubt about it, Deanna MacPartland told herself, he was a most impressive man.

She had slept with him many times by now, and not entirely without pleasure. Deanna was a healthy and attractive young woman, and Grey Thunder was a handsome and virile male. She had become a pragmatist in her brothel days, and Deanna had submitted to the Indian's caresses without a struggle. In fact, she had even derived great pleasure from their subsequent couplings. But that did not mean in any way that her love or loyalty had diminished when it came to Dave Watson.

Deanna had known the bodies of many men, but her heart belonged to one alone. Nor did the Kansan expect perfect fidelity under such conditions. They both understood the hard life of the frontier, and both believed that it was no sin to take comfort wherever they found it in the course of their hard and perilous journies. Deanna was further comforted by the thought which Dave had shared with her during the last night that she and the Kansan had spent together, under the threat of death and disaster on Long Island, menaced by savage dogs and equally savage Russian Cossacks.

All things are pure to the pure in heart. This was the gift which the Kansan had given his beloved on their last night of love. It had come from one of his Uncle Ethan's books, and Dave had never forgotten it. Nor would Deanna. She interpreted it to mean that she was justified in doing her best to survive and eventually return to the Kansan, be he crippled or whole. And if she chose to relieve the boredom, despair and bleakness of her captivity by pleasuring herself, then so be it. Her body may have been coupled with that of Grey Thunder, but in her mind and in her heart of hearts, Deanna MacPartland made love only to Dave Watson.

Pleasuring one's self in this instance was merely a way of sustaining hope and courage in a desperate situation, and Deanna engaged in lovemaking with the Cheyenne brave in order to feed and replenish herself. At no time did she ever, not for a single second, feel that she was being untrue to the Kansan. And if Dave Watson should have ever found himself in the arms of a sympathetic stranger, Deanna would not object. *What's sauce for the goose,* she believed, *is sauce for the gander.*

Suddenly, Deanna was jolted from her reverie as she heard Grey Thunder's deep voice.

"Golden Woman," he called in Cheyenne, his voice resonant and clear in the chill silence of the teepee. "Golden Woman, you are not sleeping."

She shook her head, and as she did, the firelight gleamed as it was reflected in the long strands of her light blonde hair.

"I have dreamed," Grey Thunder whispered, looking deep into her prairie flower-blue eyes. "I saw you in my dream, Golden Woman. You and I were riding across the prairie—both of us, on the back of a bull buffalo! And as I looked around, the grass and scrub bushes were all covered with blood." He shook his head. "I do not know what this means. I must go to Spotted Elk, the medicine man of my people. He will know."

Deanna stared back into the brave's dark eyes, understanding but little of what he said. But she was held by the hypnotic way in which he recited his dream, and by the underlying urgency in his tone of voice.

"We were riding along in this manner for some time, across a prairie full of bloodied grass and skulls and bones . . . of both animals and men," Grey Thunder went on. "Suddenly the bull headed down into a ravine, causing you to cry out and clutch me tightly. And I dug my hands into the fur of the buffalo as he sped down the steep slope that led to the bottom of the ravine. And then I cried out your name in warning when I saw what awaited us there."

He sat up and proceeded to throw several handfuls of buffalo chips into the fire, causing it to flare up and sputter for several moments. And once it had died down, Grey Thunder resumed his narrative.

"The buffalo stopped suddenly. It would not move anymore. And just in front of it, facing us at the bottom of the deep ravine, were many white men . . . all of them carrying big rifles and long, sharp knives." He shuddered involuntarily. "Knives like the scalping knives of the Cheyenne, but even bigger. And then you slid off the buffalo's back and moved toward the white men . . . slowly, as if you were a spirit."

There was pain in Grey Thunder's eyes now. "And then I called out to you. I called 'Golden Woman!' But you did not stop. You did not heed. And then you were in the arms of some white man."

Deanna was mesmerized by the Cheyenne's tone of voice and facial expressions, even though she could not comprehend the meaning of what he said.

"Then the whites stepped in front of you, closing ranks, and you were lost to my sight. They raised their weapons and took aim at me." Grey Thunder shuddered again. "I looked for you, but could only see the mouths of many rifles, all of them looking big as the mouths of caves. Again I called out your name, but you did not respond. And then my voice became small, and would not leave my throat. I could no longer call to you." The fire flared up momentarily and illuminated Grey Thunder's face. Deanna was startled by the pain and anxiety that she saw in his eyes.

"The whites were ready to fire their guns at me," he told her in a hollow voice. "And one of them brandished his scalping knife in the air and leered at me. I could not move. I was paralyzed, and still sat on the buffalo's back. I could not move. I was helpless."

He cleared his throat and looked down at the ground. "I knew that my time had come. But I could not even meet the enemy in battle, unarmed though I was. It was as if someone had worked a great medicine on me. A very bad medicine. It was as if a bad spirit had gotten inside of me, and was controlling my body."

Grey Thunder picked up another handful of buffalo chips and tossed it into the fire. As the flames leapt up this time, Deanna MacPartland saw beads of sweat on the warrior's brow.

"I knew that my time had come," he said once more, his voice gone suddenly husky. "But just as the leader of the white men—the man who had taken you in his arms—gave the signal to fire, everything disappeared . . . and I found myself transported to the teepee of my father." He cleared his throat. "I was a papoose, and my mother held me in her arms. And I was very happy. She sang the songs that she used to sing when I was a little boy."

The Cheyenne shook his head. "It was a very strange dream. Often dreams are prophetic." He was silent for a long time. "Perhaps I will be killed," he said haltingly. "But that is not for me to say. Only a medicine man could explain the meaning of my dreams." His eyes blazed for a moment. "Besides, it is a great honor for a Cheyenne to die in battle. There is no greater honor among our people."

Sensing the change in Grey Thunder's mood, Deanna smiled at the brave.

"And you are still here with me, Golden Woman," he told her, his eyes gleaming as they reflected the firelight. "And the enemy is still far from here. So now we will make love and forget about blood and dreams and death and white men."

The blanket fell away from Grey Thunder as he rose from the ground and came toward Deanna MacPartland, and she smiled when she saw that he already had an erection.

"Like it or not, gentlemen, we are all in the same boat. And only we can bail ourselves out, for that boat is about to founder."

These words were uttered by Duncan Stearns, as the big, red-headed Scotsman addressed his neighbors. His saloon, the Golden Slipper, was packed to the rafters with townsmen, settlers, ranchers, farmers and sheepmen; They had assembled there in response to his summons, knowing that he was about to take action with regard to the growing threat of a general Indian uprising in the surrounding country.

The big Scotsman stood atop the long hardwood bar of the Golden Slipper as he addressed the crowd. He had a reputation both as a man of action and as a man who always succeeds, and the audience in the saloon listened with respect and interest as he harangued them.

"Kansas, Nebraska, Colorado, the Texas grazing lands, the access to the railheads up north—this is our land, gentlemen, and not the Indian's. We are the force that spread civilization throughout the plains—nay, throughout this entire continent! And are we to let a pack of howling, blasphemous, baby-killing savages turn us back? Are we to let a bunch of degenerate heathen send us packing?"

"No! No!" the audience cried, with the voice of many men.

"The white race has traversed all the inhabited lands of the world—even the dark continent, Africa," Stearns went on when the cheering had died down. "Everywhere we have gone, civilization has followed. The record of history exists to prove that. And I ask you, my friends: why should anyone think for a moment that a pack of illiterate natives has the power to slow down the inexorable march of progress? It is the white man's burden to rule and elevate the lesser races of the globe. And that is the task we find before us!"

The crowd cheered again.

"In less than a month spring will be upon us, gentlemen. And you know what that means as well as I do." Here Stearns paused for effect and looked the crowd over, making eye contact with many of the individuals who composed it.

"That means the Indians will go out once more upon the plains—that the Red Scourge will be abroad in the land. And then all hell will break loose . . . because what has transpired so far, my friends, has just been the slightest glimpse of the horror the future holds in store this year if the redskins are permitted to range the plains and prairies untrammeled!"

He thrust his head forward on his bull-neck, his square jaw outthrust and a belligerent expression in his eyes. "They burnt my ranch to the ground, boys—surely you remember that!" His eyes flashed as he spoke and he clenched his huge, meaty fists. "My ranch was burned to the ground, and my cows and horses all stolen or slaughtered. And more important than that—far more important, gentlemen—is the fact that all my hands were murdered during the sneak attack. All their bodies were mutilated!"

The listeners cried out in anger and protest at his mention of the attack and its consequences. It was some time before Duncan Stearns could make himself heard again.

"My ranch was not so far from where we stand today, my friends," he thundered. "My place was only ten miles north of Hays City! And to the Indians, who roam the plains far and wide, all your places are not far. All of them stand well within raiding distance." His eyes flashed again, and the Scotsman drew himself up to his full height.

"And you had better look to the safety of your wives and little ones!" Duncan Stearns said in a voice that filled the large room. "For there was a lass at my ranch—a guest of mine—who was taken into captivity by the Indians."

At this, a great hubbub arose from the crowd, and the men who had come to hear Stearns exchanged angry and outraged looks.

"This lass, who was barely more than twenty years old, was stolen by the fiend known as Grey Thunder—the Cheyenne renegade who has been terrorizing West Kansan and East Colorado. She was at my place on a visit," he lied, "having been brought there by her uncle. And that man was a lifelong friend of mine," Stearns lied once more, referring to the late John Hartung. "Do you know what happened to that good and honest man, gentlemen?" he asked, narrowing his eyes and putting his hands on his hips.

"What happened to 'im, Dunc?" an old rancher asked.

"He was butchered and scalped," the Scotsman said in a voice both quiet and arresting at the same time. "There wasn't much left of poor John by the time that we reached the ranch." He shook his head and smiled malevolently at his listeners. "Do you lads want your wives and wee babes to be food for the crows? Or even worse . . . do you want them taken captive by those unspeakable barbarians? Is that what you men want?"

"No! No!" roared the crowd, agitated and angry. *"No, by God! We do not!"*

"Well then," Stearns roared back several minutes

later, shouting over the voices of the men in the Golden Slipper Saloon, "You had better do something about those red bastards, now, hadn't you?"

"Yes! Yes!" howled the crowd as Duncan Stearns played with their emotions and manipulated them like marionettes. *"We will! Damn right, we will!"*

"Then listen to me, and I'll tell you what Duncan Stearns is going to do," the redheaded giant bellowed back at the crowd. "I'm going to round up as many good men as I can—be it ten or a hundred—and go out and settle the score with Grey Thunder and any other hostiles who have the great misfortune to cross our path!"

The men in the saloon all cheered wildly at this.

"I've been out with a few hands in late autumn," he resumed when things had quieted down. "And I've already left my calling cards with the savages." Here he paused to grin wolfishly down at his listeners. "And I've even collected a few keepsakes." And then, dramatically, Stearns extended his long arm and pointed to the rear of the Golden Slipper.

"Show 'em what we brought back from our last little outing, Crawford!" he called out.

At the rear of the saloon the scar-faced, curly-headed man who had gunned down the half-breed scout, Tolliver, stood up from the table where he had been sitting. Grinning from ear to ear, Crawford raised a stick into the air, holding it parallel to the ground. A murmur went up from the crowd as it became apparent that at least eight or nine scalps hung from that stick. All of them had come from persons with very dark hair, although two were streaked with grey, and three had belonged to children.

Cheers went up from the agitated men in the saloon.

"That's what I've already done," Duncan Stearns bellowed over the dying roar of his audience. "And that's only a taste of what I intend to do!"

"By God, Duncan you're the boy to do it!" cried a bald-headed rancher below Stearns

"Give 'em hell, Dunc!" a settler yelled.

"Count me in!" hollered a sheepman.

"Me too!" seconded a short, fat rancher. *"An' all my boys! We'll back ya up, all right, Duncan!"*

"Damn right!" someone yelled. *"We're right beside ya!"*

"You can count on us, Duncan!" yet another man bellowed, with other voices rising at the same time.

"Kill them red dogs!"

"Clear them sum'bitches off'n the plains!"

"Let's ride out with Duncan an' git that damn Grey Thunder's scalp!"

"Death to all Injuns! Shoot 'em all dead!"

"Wipe 'em all out—every last one if 'em! Man, woman an' child!"

The crowd moved like an insane thing swaying back and forth in the dark intoxication of rage and blood-lust, its component elements in motion, giving it the look of some great beast rippling its muscles.

"This is our chance, gentlemen!" Duncan Stearns called out exultantly when the mob finally began to quiet-down. "The Army's had its chance . . . now it's ours."

"Them nigger cavalrymen ain't done diddley-shit 'bout the stichiayshun," an old settler with a two-foot-long white beard grumbled.

"What can y'all expect from a pack of nigras?" a

man with a deep-South accent drawled at the top of his voice.

"Well, never mind the blackies!" Duncan Stearns roared, reasserting his hold over the crowd at the Golden Slipper. "This is white man's work! And it's white men I'm calling for to do it, by God! Never mind the U.S. Cavalry—the Army's at skeleton strength throughout the West, and it can't make the difference. You all know that!"

"Damn right we do!"

"They ain't been wuff a shit since the War between the States!"

"An' who needs them damn used-to-be slaves fightin' fer white folks! We can take care of our own!"

"Us whites can put them damn redskins in their place!"

This sentiment was voiced so strongly that any potential defenders of the black troopers, the U.S. Cavalry, and the U.S. Army refrained from speaking out. Stearns had already whipped his audience to fever pitch, transforming them from an interested crowd into a rabid and bloodthirsty mob. Those opposed to him saw that discretion was the better part of valor, for any one who had the temerity to object to the Scotsman's proposals would surely have been lynched or beaten to death for his pains.

"Well, gentlemen," Stearns cried out, "what's it to be? Are you going to continue to let those murderous heathen prey upon you and your families? Are you going to let them continue to rob you blind and live off the fruits of *your* labors? Are you going to let them dictate to white men?" He paused for emphasis here, looking out into the crowd, challenging every man-jack of them with his flashing and icy blue eyes. *"Or are you going to ride out beside Duncan Stearns and put an end to the murderous and thieving savages once and for all?"*

The mob went wild at this, and it was a full ten minutes before the big Scotsman could speak again.

"Gentlemen," he boomed, holding his big, thick-fingered hands up in the air, "I just want to thank you all for your neighborly support and your vote of confidence. I'll keep you informed of the plans, and I welcome all your suggestions and information. In a month or so, we'll all ride out of Hays City together and settle the 'Indian problem' in this country once and for all." He lowered his hands and smiled at his listeners. "And now, my friends, belly up to the bar—the drinks are on me!"

Whooping and hollering with glee at this news, the men in the Golden Slipper stampeded toward the bar. After they had all been served, the senior rancher present called them to attention and raised his glass aloft.

"Gentleman, I give you Duncan Stearns," he called out in a sandpaper voice. "A born leader and a man who knows how to deal with them red devils!"

"Duncan Stearns!" the crowd roared. *"Cheers!"*

Stearns, his cold eyes suddenly warmed by a glow of triumph, raised his glass and then knocked back his drink in one gulp.

After the toast the men all sang *For He's a Jolly Good Fellow,* as the big redhead made his way up to his office on the landing above the saloon floor. And after he had entered the office of his partner, Bert Freckleton, drinks were served once again, and for a long time for a long time thereafter.

Duncan Stearns had a demonic smile upon his lips and a fierce gleam in his executioner's eyes as he entered the office and sauntered up to Bert Freckleton's desk.

"Och, if ye keep up that kind o' talk, laddie," the scrawny, wizened man who was Stearns' partner told the exultant Scot; "ye'll be a sairtainty for-r-r the gov'norship. I can tell ye that much." He reached into a polished wooden box on his desk and pulled out two big cigars.

"It's off to Topeka ye'll be, Duncan," Freckleton went on, handing one of the cigars to Stearns, who sat down by the opposite side of the desk. "They wer-r-re all in the palm of yer hand tonight."

Stearns bit off the end of the cigar and spat it into Bert Freckleton's wastebasket. Then he pulled a Lucifer out of his vest pocket and flicked his thumbnail against it. As the sulphur of the match flared, he puffed upon his cigar and cocked an eye at his parter.

"Bertie, my boy." he grunted, still puffing the stogie alight, "what we do this spring is going to take me all the way to the governor's mansion." He took the cigar out of his mouth. "Then we'll be on easy street . . . and those bloody redskins will have put us there." He smiled at the other man.

"In fact, we should be grateful to that bastard, Grey Thunder, for that laddie's the one who's made all this possible. He's given us the most burning issue on the frontier. And in Hays City and the outlying territory, we've got just the means to resolve it."

"Och, haie!" Freckleton exclaimed. "Ye've got those boys mor-r-re than r-r-r-ready to go out after Indian scalps—tha's fer sairtain!"

"It's not just Indian scalps I'm after, Bertie," Duncan Stearns told his partner, the smile fading from his lips. "I intend to get that MacPartland lass back and take her with me to Topeka."

"Aye, she'll no' tur-r-rn her nose up at the governor's mansion. No lass in her r-r-right mind would!"

"Aye, she'll come along, right enough," Stearns agreed. "I've no question about that, once I've accomplished my primary purpose."

"And what might that be?" Bert Freckleton asked.

"My primary purpose in this whole business is still what it was at the outset," the redhead giant told him. "To put that Watson bastard six feet under the ground!"

7

RIDERS ON THE PLAINS

The weeks dragged on for the Kansan. The long winter had been made bearable only by the presence of so many friends and loved ones in the Pawnee camp—Marcus Haverstraw, and Soaring Hawk; his many good friends among the Pawnee warriors, and the wise and kindly chief, Running Buffalo. And there was the one person who made the ache of his loss and the cold pain of his loneliness disappear for a time, the one person who loved the Kansan and gave herself to him totally—Bright Water. But he would be leaving her soon, never to return.

He knew that and she knew that; and as the Kansan sat with the warriors and elders of the Pawnees, in the tent of Chief Running Buffalo, his Indian sweetheart was much on his mind. He would miss her very much, Dave Watson was certain of that. But they both accepted the way things were to be, even though it would grieve her to know that the Kansan was going to be reunited with his white beloved or die in the attempt.

It was with a heavy heart and mixed feelings that the Kansan made his preparations to ride out of the Pawnee camp. But, he told himself, feeling a sharp pang of guilt every time he thought about Bright Water, a man had to do what he had to do. He had his trail, and there was nothing for him to do but follow it. If he did not, he would never know a moment's peace or self-respect again. It was that simple.

"Now that you will be riding out, we must ask our new medicine man, Night Hawk, to make good medicine in honor of your departure," Running Buffalo told the Kansan, drawing him out of his thoughts. "I will send for him." Saying this, the chief nodded to one of the young men, who rose immediately and left the big tent.

"In the old days things were very different," the old chief continued. "In the days before we became the good friends of the white man, the spring season was greeted in a far different manner than it is now." He cleared his throat and looked around at his listeners, all of whom, the Kansan included, were anxious to hear his tales of how the Pawnee had lived long ago.

"When I was a boy," Running Buffalo told his listeners, "the Pawnees still performed the rite of the Captive Girl Sacrifice. They did this so that the corn and other crops would grow tall, and that the buffalo would continue to roam the plains. This sacrifice was given up to Morning Star, who gave men light and warmth when she mated with Evening Star."

Some of the older Pawnees nodded, sharing the chief's memories and knowledge of tribal lore.

"For four days the tribe prepared itself, with purification, fasting and restraint from the coming together of men and women," Running Buffalo said. "Medicine was made at this time, as the Pawnees prepared for the coming of the spring. And when this period had concluded, a war-party left the camp.

"What these warriors searched for was a girl who was just about to become a woman. To obtain one, they would attack the camp of one of our enemies and carry the girl off. She was brought back to our camp and treated with much honor. The women rubbed her with perfumes that were special to the occasion. She was dressed in the finest clothing and adorned with feathers, beads and bone. This girl was fed the best delicacies in the camp, such as buffalo tongue and buffalo hump. She stayed as a most honored guest until the day came to perform the special ceremony in honor of Morning Star."

He paused to pick his nose, a thoughtful expression upon his face as he did.

"At that time, men were sent to bring back four special types of wood—elm and elder, willow and cottonwood. These were used to build a scaffold for the sacred rite, and each represented both a direction," he pointed toward the north, east, south and west in turn, "and one of the sacred animals." Here he looked at the Kansan, "Bear, wildcat, wolf and mountain lion. The scaffold would be built the day before the great ceremony, and the girl would be conducted to it shortly before the break of day.

"The night before, the women will all paint the body of this pure young girl. Black was the color they painted her left side, for that is the color of night. Her right side was painted red, for that is both the color of the day and the Morning Star. The girl wore a painted buffalo hide as she was led to the scaffold. The medicine men smoked tobacco and offered it up, along with prayers and chants, before an altar. The whole tribe—young and old, men and women—sang along with the medicine men.

"Four of the medicine men led the young girl to the scaffold, and then tied her spread-eagled to its framework. And when the first ray of the Morning Star shone down upon the earth, a chosen warrior came forth and sent an arrow through the heart of the Captive Girl. After that, another warrior cut open her breast with a sacred knife made of flint. He daubed his face with her blood, as it ran down her body, finally dripping on an offering of choicest buffalo meat placed below the scaffold."

The old chief cleared his throat and blew his nose.

"The four men who had originally bound the girl cut her down once she was dead. They took the body out on the prairie, a quarter of a mile to the east of the camp, where they left it, face-down upon the ground. And as they went, they sang: 'The whole earth she shall turn into. The whole earth shall receive her blood. She will turn into a bunch of grass. The ants will find her. The moths will come and find her: The fox will come and find her as will the coyote, the wildcat, the magpie, the crow. Buzzards will come and find her. And last of all will be the bald-headed eagle, who will come and eat her.'

"After the four medicine men had returned to the village, they and the other direct participants in the great ceremony went to the earth lodge to eat the buffalo meat that had been made sacred by the blood of the Captive Girl. At the same time, the rest of the tribe engaged in a mighty celebration. The things that they did were to sing and dance as they rejoiced, to praise

Morning Star and Mother Corn, and to have each other—men and women—to ensure that the earth would be fertile once more."

Running Buffalo shook his head slowly. "That was long ago. Once a warrior named Man Chief, the son of the big chief whose name was Knife Chief, tried to put an end to the great ceremony when he untied the girl, put her on a pony, and told her to ride like the wind toward her people. And soon, the whites forced us to abandon this ancient practice, this custom that has come down from time beyond remembering."

There was a wistful smile upon the chief's leathery old face as he said his next words. "But the world was a better place in those days. Things went better for our people back in the days when we killed the Captive Girl. The earth was happy then." He shook his head. "It is no longer pleased with us." He raised his hand and held it to his heart. "This I know."

The Kansan stared at Running Buffalo, as the old Pawnee grew silent and lowered his head. He and Marcus and their Pawnee allies, led by Soaring Hawk, would ride out in the morning, searching for Grey Thunder. And in a short time, Dave Watson was convinced, the earth would not lack for blood.

A bugle sounded in the morning air, loud and clear, and the heavy wooden gates to Fort Kingston swung open slowy with the sound of creaking hinges and groaning wood. Inside the army post a voice called out a series of commands, and the Tenth Cavalry began to walk their horses through the gate. The regimental band was playing.

The troopers had reformed outside the fort, and their commanding officer rode by the ranks, inspecting the black cavalrymen and their mounts. When the inspection was over, the commanding officer saluted the sergeants who sat on horseback in front of the ranks. They returned his salute and immediately began to bawl out a series of orders as the officer wheeled his horse around and walked it toward the open plain.

An instant later, the black troopers began to follow him in formation, a sergeant at the head of each cavalry squadron. The regimental band could once again be heard from within the fort. This time it was playing *Garryowen,* the tune that George Armstrong Custer's regimental band had played during the winter massacre of Black Kettle's Cheyenne on the Washita River.

It was springtime now, and whatever grim associations with the hardships of a winter campaign that the tune possesses were lost upon the black troopers; for instead of the snows and ice of that terrible expedition, the sun shone brightly overhead and a warm zephyr had come up from the south. The cavalrymen themselves were glad to escape for the moment at least from the confinement of Fort Kingston and the tedious, humdrum round of spit-and-polish inspections and makework which characterized an army at peace.

With but one exception, the force was composed entirely of black men. Riding at the head of the long blue column was Lieutenant Peter J. McCluskey, a Boston Irishman who had risen from the ranks of distinguishing himself in the Union Army. McCluskey had been brevetted to the rank of major by the beginning of the great conflict's fourth year; but after the Civil War, when the Army was pared to the bone, the Irishman was given the rank of First Lieutenant.

McCluskey was an officer who cared for his troops, and was in turn much liked by them. Unlike many officers, he was comfortable drinking with his men, be they black or white. He was as shrewd as he was valorous, and had earned the respect of his men by avoiding situations where they would be called upon to unnecessarily risk their lives. In this most important mater he differed from leaders such as Custer, or even Napoleon Bonaparte, both of whom were extremely prodigal of the lives of their soldiers.

Having served in the Southwest and on the Great Plains since the Civil War had ended, Lieutenant McCluskey had become an experienced Indian fighter. It was in this capacity that he and his troopers sallied forth from Fort Kingston. It was imperative that they locate Grey Thunder and his band of hostiles before the sparks which had been struck by the Cheyenne's actions set the prairies and plains ablaze with the conflagration of an Indian war.

To this end, Lieutenant McCluskey had carefully chosen his scouts, knowing from bitter experience how difficult it was to track and catch an Indian on the move. Working on the assumption that it takes an Indian to catch an Indian, McCluskey had brought with him a number of Crow scouts. The Crow were the hereditary enemies of the Cheyenne, as were the Pawnee, whom Frank North had used so effectively against Grey Thunder's people, and so McCluskey thought to do the same with the eight Crows he had recruited for the mission. They were led by a stern warrior named Howling Dog, a veteran of many years' combat with the Cheyenne. This was the lieutenant's ace in the hole; and this was why the commanding officer of Fort Kingston had approved McCluskey's plan to nip Grey Thunder's springtime depredations in the bud. The Irishman was filled with confidence as he and the troopers of the Tenth rode smartly out of the army post, but it is doubtful if he would have remained so optimistic if he had known that Duncan Stearns and a civilian force, as well as the Kansan and his Pawnee allies, were also out on the plains in search of Grey Thunder and Deanna MacPartland.

"I'm paying five dollars for every Indian scalp that we bring back to Hays City when this business is all over, gentlemen," Duncan Stearns told the men who rode out of the frontier town with him, all of them headed on what appeared to be a collision course with the Cheyenne renegade who had been terrorizing the country. It was do-or-die now, and the men who came along with the big Scotsman were determined to end the "Indian problem" in their vicinity once and for all.

The force of armed horsemen who rode out of Hays City on that first spring morning of 1871 was composed of more than sixty men. Nearly fifty of the riders were ranchers, cowhands, settlers and citizens whom Duncan Stearns had persuaded to accompany him on his grim mission of extermination. The remaining horsemen were the Hays City roughs and desperadoes who had first ridden out with him, and who now constituted what amounted to the Scotman's private police force. These hard cases were kept in line by the conscienceless killer known as Crawford, the scar-faced and curly-headed desperado who had become Stearn's right-hand man.

Crawford had killed the half-breed, Tolliver, on Stearns' orders, shooting him in the back and showing no more compunction than a boy tearing the wings off a dragonfly. He had already killed well over half a dozen men in his time, and was not at all modest about that grim tally. Crawford had not been in town when the Kansan and his friends shot up the redheaded giant's saloon, but he assured the Scotsman that he would make short work of both Bill Cody and Bill Hickok, if either of those bravos happened to cross his path in the future. And as for Dave Watson, the hired killer knew that Duncan Stearns would allow no man to deprive him of the pleasure of killing the Kansan with his own hands.

The big redhead wore a lopsided grin as he rode at the head of his small army. He had much to look forward to in the days ahead, Stearns told himself, and he was certain that his imminent accomplishments would contribute heavily toward establishing him as the most powerful man in the entire state of Kansas.

In a short time he would eliminate Grey Thunder and his band of hostiles, and Stearns had determined to ride back into Hays City bearing as many Indian scalps as he and his bully-boys could lay their hands upon. It did not matter whether the scalps in question came from women and children; it would be more than sufficient that they came from Indians of any kind. The more scalps the expedition brought back, the more visible proof that he, Duncan Stearns, had dealt effectively with the Indian menace throughout the southern plains.

Once he had dealt with Grey Thunder, the Scotsman knew that he would automatically acquire Deanna MacPartland. This thought pleased him immensely, for Stearns was obsessed with the thought of possessing the blonde beauty, and he had made up his mind to take her with him to the state house after his anticipated triumph. But his greatest triumph lay elsewhere.

That would come only when Duncan Stearns came face to face once more with Dave Watson. He had suffered a great humiliation at the Kansan's hands—a humiliation which could only be expunged with the man's blood. Stearns would not rest until he had shot Dave Watson down like a mad dog, or torn him apart with his bare hands. He had been patient so far, biding his time until he next encountered the Kansan; and he was certain that his patience would soon be rewarded.

Before long, he told himself, his path and the Kansan's would cross again. *And when it did, he would be ready to take his revenge.*

On the morning after Duncan Stearns and his forces had ridden out of Hays City, Dave Watson, Marcus Haverstraw, Soaring Hawk and fifteen Pawnee warriors left Running Buffalo's camp as the sun rose in the east. The Kansan took one backward look as he rode away, and he felt a sharp pang of guilt at the thought of parting from the young squaw who had been his lover over the latter half of the winter.

Tall and straight as a young sapling, the woman stood at the edge of the Pawnee camp and watched the Kansan ride off, never turning away until her sharp eyes could no longer distinguish the riders' forms in the distance. The woman made no sound nor moved a muscle. When she finally turned away, there were tears in Bright Water's eyes. But at the very same time that she shed those tears, the young Pawnee experienced a rapturous feeling of relief, one that filled her with a profound sense of acceptance.

The Kansan was gone, she told herself, and nothing that Bright Water could do would alter that fact. It was the end of her years of love, of her painful and hopeless love for Dave Watson. It was ended, and he was leaving; he would either be reunited with the white woman he loved, or die in the attempt. And that was that, Bright Water told herself, sniffling and wiping her eyes as she turned back to the camp of her people.

It was over, she kept repeating to herself. It was over. And as she did this, Bright Water began to feel a sudden gladness. She knew that she was now free to get on with her own life. As she wiped her eyes once more, walking briskly back into Running Buffalo's camp, Bright Water began to giggle quietly, when she realized that she had been smiling.

Grey Thunder drew his Winchester rifle out of its boot, grasped it by the stock, and then worked the rifle's lever, sending a cartridge into the firing chamber as he peered at the distant forms of horsemen coming toward him from the Northwest. The other Cheyenne warriors with him all did the same thing, holding their various weapons at the ready while they, too, stared at the dust cloud up ahead.

"They are not white men," Running Antelope told his brother, having the sharpest eyes among all the braves. "Their horses are too small. These men ride ponies."

"Yes, I can see that now," Grey Thunder murmured, staring hard at the tiny figures on the horizon.

"These men are Indians," Running Antelope said with conviction.

"That is so," his brother agreed a moment later.

Then a silence fell upon the small band of horsemen, as they waited patiently until the approaching Indians could be identified as either friends or foe. The sun shone brightly overhead, and the first flowers of spring dotted the prairie.

"Those men are Sioux," Running Antelope said presently, breaking the silence. "Lakota Sioux."

"It is good," rumbled Grey Thunder. "They are good friends to the Cheyenne. Perhaps they have come to join us."

The thunder of hoofbeats soon became audible, and the long, fur-wrapped braids and bright feathers of the Sioux braves could be seen clearly through the cloud of dust raised by the riders. There were thirteen of them, all warriors, all fairly young men. The Cheyennes could make out the weapons in their hands now, as well as the decorations and dress of the oncoming horsemen. The rider at the head of the party whooped and began to wave his rifle over his head, calling out Grey Thunder's name as he did. Once he had calmed down again, the brave signalled the riders behind him to slow their pace, and he reined in his own pony and took the remaining several hundred yards at a walk.

"It is Tall Elk," Grey Thunder observed, nodding as he spoke, a thin smile of satisfaction flickering onto his lips. "He has come to be with us once more."

Walking his horse to the Cheyennes, with his band following, the big Sioux thrust his rifle into its boot and straightened up on the back of his dappled pony. And the the man raised his hands and began to communicate with Grey Thunder by way of sign language.

"Why does he do that?" wondered Running Antelope. "Tall Elk speaks the language of the Cheyenne."

"It means that some of the braves who are with him do not," Grey Thunder told his brother, raising his hand to return the Sioux's open-palmed sign of peace. "Just as most of our people do not speak the language of other Indians, so it is with the Sioux. Men were given different languages by the Great Spirit. That is the way things are in the world."

Few Indian tribes on the Great Plains shared a common tongue, and therefore the highly-developed sign language served as a universal mode of communcation. While this manual language admitted of local variants and idiosyncrasies, it was, by and large, basically understood by all Indians, whether on the plains or in the desert, in the mountains or by the seacoasts, in the great forests or the lake country.

It is good to see my friend, Grey Thunder, again. Tall Elk signalled as he drew near to the waiting band. *The Lakota salute the Cheyenne.*

The Cheyenne salute the worthy Sioux, Grey Thunder signalled back as the horsemen of both bands looked on. *What brings my good friend Tall Elk back to this country?*

I have come back to join Grey Thunder and his warriors, as I promised when the winter started.

You are welcome among us, my friend. And so are your brother Sioux.

This time I have brought twelve braves with me, all of them worthy warriors among our people. They are happy to fight beside our good friends, the Cheyenne.

It is good, signalled Grey Thunder, a solemn expression upon his face as he raised his right arm and placed his closed fist over his heart, tapping his chest three times. *My heart is glad. There is much work to be done this season. There are many whites to be killed. . . .*

"Well, here we go again," Marcus Haverstraw said cheerfully as he rode beside the Kansan, "charging full-tilt into the gasping jaws of death and destruction."

Dave Watson grinned at his friend. "You sure got one hell of a colorful way of sayin' that we're 'bout to risk our butts another time, Marcus."

"It lends the trappings of poetry to the grim scaffolding of reality," the newspaperman replied, grinning back at the Kansan.

"Yep, I reckon if ya got to go," Dave agreed, "it's a heap better to go with a little poetry behind ya. Why, them words of yours'd look plumb elegant on yer tombstone, ol' hoss."

The journalist flashed him a creaky smile and looked past the Kansan to Soaring Hawk, who rode on Dave's other side.

"How about you, Mister Hawk?" he asked the Pawnee. "What d'you think of my way of looking at our latest adventure?"

"White men bullshit too much," Soaring Hawk remarked coming directly to the point, his expressionless features turned toward Marcus P. Haverstraw. "It is easier to find talking white fox than quiet white man."

The Kansan guffawed at this. "Any other questions, perfessor?" he asked the newspaperman.

"In my natural state of exuberance I chanced to overlook the inbred taciturnity of our aboriginal friends, old man," Marcus told Dave Watson. "I will not contest the issue. It is said that 'Silence is golden,' and I must therefore consider, according to that time-honored adage, that our friend Mister Hawk is an extremely wealthy man."

The Kansan turned to regard the Connecticut journalist. "I don't know what the hell yer talkin' 'bout."

Marcus sighed. "I was merely addressing myself to the practice of silence, and its attendant virtues."

"Well, actions speak louder'n words," the Kansan reminded him.

They rode on in silence for some time, Dave, Marcus, Soaring Hawk and the fifteen Pawnee braves who had accompanied them into the foothills of Colorado's Piedmont, the country into which they had tracked Grey Thunder and his band of hostiles. Somewhere in this rugged country, where men and horses were easily hidden, Soaring Hawk and the Pawnees who had scouted for Major Frank North felt they would once more encounter their old enemies, the Cheyenne.

From the tracks which they had been following, the Pawnees estimated that there were now over thirty braves in Grey Thunder's band. That figure had been arrived at without counting the tracks of the spare ponies and the horses which bore the women. The tracks of these were always accompanied by the scars of the group's several travois, which were pulled by the camp dogs. But the tracks of the raiders were distinguished each time they diverged from the general assembly.

This had happened several times already, between Kansas and Colorado, and each time the Kansan and the Pawnees followed this second trail, it almost inevitably led to the scene of some recent disaster. The band of hostiles had last raided the stagecoach depot at Butterick, a small settlement in the northeastern part of Colorado, and burned it to the ground. Judging from the tracks of the ponies that rode away from Butterick, the Pawnee scouts believed that the raiders were somewhere in the vicinity in which they now travelled. And they were in full force, which meant that there were at least two Cheyenne or Sioux for each man who rode with Dave Watson and Soaring Hawk. The time for a showdown was drawing near.

Although the Kansan and his party were outnumbered two to one, that fact made little impression upon Dave Watson. He had originally intended to set out after Grey Thunder by himself until Marcus Haverstraw joined him, and now the presence of his blood-brother and fifteen trail-savvy, Cheyenne-battling Pawnees made the Kansan feel as if he were at the head of an army. He could ask for no better companions as he went hunting for the Cheyenne and his band. They were rapidly closing in on Grey Thunder, and it was only a matter of time before he would come face to face with the brave who had taken Deanna MacPartland.

With a lighter heart than he had known for the past year, Dave Watson sat by the campfire and made plans with his Indian trailmates. However they came to encounter Grey Thunder and his warriors, Dave and his allies all agreed that Deanna MacPartland should be rescued from the Cheyenne's camp only when the main force of the hostiles was adjudged to be far from the site. In this manner the Kansan would be able to enter the lightly guarded camp by stealth and free Deanna at no great risk to her safety, while the Pawnees created a diverion and then attacked the few men who remained to defend the place.

"I reckon I'm gon' turn in early," Dave Watson told the others as he rose and began to unroll his blanket. "I got to rest up fer when I git to see my gal." He chuckled and beamed at the men who sat by the blazing fire. "She's gon' be right surprised to see me."

Suddenly his smile went sharp and cold as a Pawnee's scalping knife. "An' so's that Cheyenne sum'bitch, Grey Thunder!"

"Great God in Zion!" Corporal Homer White cried suddenly. "Do you see what I see?"

"Well, I'll be a blue-balled muleskinner!" was Sergeant Wardell Bumstead's reply when he saw what his companion was pointing at.

What had so surprised the two black troopers was the group of horsemen that came riding toward them in the Colorado hills, a group of sixty white civilians headed by a redheaded giant of a man. The cavalry squadrons which had left Fort Kingston behind Lieutenant Peter J. McCluskey were now camped at the foot of a large hill, and the men were just cooking their breakfast in silence, since the Crow scouts had made it known the day before that the hostiles were near.

"Jaysus, Mary an' Joseph!" Lieutenant McCluskey swore as he rose to his feet and dashed the rest of his strong black coffee into the flames of the campfire. Then he held his hands up in the air and strode toward the approaching horsemen, who came toward the encampment from an easterly direction, the figures of the men and their horses silhouetted by the sun which had begun to rise behind them.

As the squat and bandy-legged cavalry officer stumped toward him, Duncan Stearns held up his right hand, signalling his party to rein in their horses.

"An' jist who in the name of Almighty God might yez all be?" Peter J. McCluskey asked, a tone of annoyance roughening his already hoarse baritone.

"We are citizens of Kansas, Colorado, and Nebraska," the big Scotsman shot back. "And we are here to hunt down the hostiles who have been raiding our settlements, murdering our people and destroying our property. My name is Stearns, and I am in charge of this expedition."

The veteran cavalryman's eyebrows went up when he heard the name, and it was plain that he was aware of Duncan Stearns' importance and influence in Kansas and the area of the southern plains.

"If ye ask me, Mister Stearns," Lieutenant McCluskey rasped, "that's a task best left to the United States Army."

Stearns lowered his cold blue eyes until they met the Irishman's brown and warmer pair. A sneer came to his lips, and he spoke in a low, even voice that was filled with contempt.

"We figure differently, Lieutenant," Stearns told McCluskey, looking past him at the black troopers in the camp. "We figure this is white man's work."

"I think yer missin' the point, sir" the Irishman growled, his eyes narrowing as he spoke. "Them lads of mine has been trained at some length to hunt Indians. Their color don't alter the fact that they are the best damned bunch of Indian fighters on the southern plains."

The desperado known as Crawford walked his horse up beside that of Duncan Stearns, who turned his head in the man's direction. Then the hired killer leaned forward in his saddle and let fly a gob of tobacco juice which splattered upon a stone not two feet from Lieutenant McCluskey's dusty brown boots.

The Irishman's face was beet-red now, and he was breathing heavily as he looked from Crawford to Stearns.

"The point is that we're out to collect some scalps, Lieutenant," Duncan Stearns growled. "So, I'll be obliged if you'll desist from any further interference in our plans."

"Ah, ya will, will ya?" the cavalryman muttered angrily, glaring up at the redheaded giant. "Now, look here, Mister," he said, wiping his nose with the back of his hand. "I'll have ya know that me an' my lads has been trackin' them hostiles fer the past few days. Why, if you an' that bunch of fellas goes in now, ye'll flush the bastards out, an' they'll hightail it outta here." He shot Duncan Stearns a look of appeal. "Now, you can understand that, can't ya, Mister?"

"What I *do* understand, Lieutenant," Stearns replied coldly, "is that you have no authority whatsoever over my party. And I'll thank you to mind your own business."

"Bedad, but yer lookin' fer trouble. If yez push on an' blunder smack into the midst of a trap, well, don't say that Peter J. McCluskey didn't warn yez," the Irishman growled. "Them hills is crawlin' with Indians fer fair."

"That's exactly why we came here, soldier," Duncan Stearns shot back. "And we've got Indian guides to lead us to the Cheyenne. He flicked the reins, urging his horse forward suddenly and causing Lieutenant McCluskey to swear and step backward out of its path.

"Ahh, may the Lord have mercy on yer soul, ya bloody idjit!" the Irishman muttered angrily as he watched the armed horsemen ride past the encampment of the Tenth Cavalry.

"Well, what do you think about that shit!" exclaimed Wardell Bumstead, as he stood up in the center of the encampment and watched the riders make their way around the base of the hill and disappear behind the farthest sentry.

"I think," replied Homer White, standing up beside the burly sergeant, "that life's gon' git damn excitin' fer them white boys pretty soon."

Wardell Bumstead shook his head and sighed. "You ain't shittin', Brother Homer. An' I ain't so sure it's gon' be the kind of action them rednecks is expectin'."

8

DEATH STALKS THE FOOTHILLS

Suddenly, in the heart of the night, the Kansan was awakened by the roar of gunfire. His eyes opened wide as he sat up, and his hard, muscular body was bathed in sweat. He shuddered, forcing himself to gulp and catch his breath, falling silent a moment later as he strained to determine where the sounds had originated. But all that Dave Watson could hear were the muted snores of Marcus Haverstraw.

No further sounds came to his ears through the inky blackness of the moonless Colorado night. "Judas Priest," the Kansan muttered, lying back down and resting his head upon his saddle, coming to the sudden awareness that the gunshots which awakened him had come from inside his own head. He had been dreaming again.

The Kansan's dreams had been wild, violent and sensuous for the past few weeks, full of passionate women and bloodthirsty Indians. And as the recollection of what he had just dreamed came flooding back at him, Dave realized that he had awakened from a dream which recurred frequently since he and Marcus had gone out on the trail at the end of the past autumn. It was the horrible dream in which the Kansan relived the ambush and massacre at Eagle Pass, when the Chiricahua Apaches had slaughtered the Cavalry expedition led by Major Jock Forbes, raining bullets, boulders and arrows down upon the hapless riders. And Dave Watson had ridden among that ill-fated troop, as he sat in chains astride his horse, the prisoner of the U.S. Army, back in the hard days when he and Soaring Hawk had crossed the arid stretches of the Southwest.

Soaring Hawk, out of sympathy for the suffering of a fellow Indian, had rescued an Apache brave and his companion from the Phoenix jailhouse, literally stealing them from under the nose of Paul Hutzelman, the vicious bounty hunter known as Killer-of-Apaches. But when it became known that the Kansan was associated with Soaring Hawk, the bounty hunter seized him in the Pawnee's stead, turning Dave over to Major Forbes, the commander of nearby Fort Burnside.

Major Jock Forbes was determined to wipe out the Apache to the last man, woman and child, and he took Dave Watson into the field with him, for use as either hostage or decoy. But the officer's plans were foiled, as the Apaches got word of his expedition and rode out to intercept it. The Apache whom Soaring Hawk had liberated turned out to be none other than the infamous Geronimo, and he caught the cavalry troop in a deadly ambush at a place know to the Chiricahuas as Eagle Pass. Only a handful of cavalrymen survived that bloody encounter, but the Kansan was rescued by Soaring Hawk and the Apaches.

"Judas Priest!" Dave Watson muttered, the scars on his back aching momentarily as he relived his earlier fifty lashes at the army post. But then the Kansan smiled as the image of a young woman sprang up in his mind's eye. It was the image of Consuela Delgado, the dark-eyed and passionate *Mexicana* who had been his lover in the new settlement of Phoenix.

"Oh, my," he groaned, shifting his position on the hard ground and drawing the saddle blanket up to his chin. "Good ol' Consuela," Dave sighed, his eyelids closing. A moment later, the Kansan was asleep.

He dreamed again: not of pain this time, but of pleasure, of the pleasures of the flesh. The Kansan was back in Phoenix again, in the house of Darrel Duppa, the Englishman who had renamed the place after it had risen from the ashes of its former incarnation as the settlement called Swillings.

The Kansan was in one of Duppa's guest rooms, and he was not alone. Standing across the room from him, naked as a jaybird, was Consuela Delgado, the woman who served as the Englishman's housekeeper. She had been much taken with the Kansan and, as a consequence, had come to him in the night.

Dave moaned and squirmed at the vision of the lovely Mexicana's long, slender limbs and glistening brown skin, her trim flanks and gently swelling hips, the full swell of her dark-nippled breasts. He could see the lamplight reflected in her night-black hair and wide, dark eyes as she came toward him.

He moaned again as the woman came into his arms, and he held her warm, supple body against him. Her smile was bright then, and the Kansan shivered lightly as her long fingernails grazed the flesh of his pectorals, running down through the dense thicket of dark blond hair upon his chest. And he, in turn, ran his big hand over her flank, across her small belly and then down through the thick black forest below, until his deft and questing fingers encountered the moaning woman's nether lips.

Ay, querido, Consuela gasped as the Kansan's middle finger slid between those swollen and throbbing outer lips. She pressed herself closer to him, threw back her head, shut her eyes, and opened her full-lipped mouth slightly.

He leaned forward to meet her, and they kissed, his finger still making the light, gliding runs which caused the Latin beauty to shudder and gasp with delight. Their tongues met in teasing, salamandrine play, as their lips firmly pressed together. Consuela Delgado squirmed and moaned as Dave Watson continued to ply the intimate vulvic caress, her passion rising like a prairie fire with a high wind behind it.

With one hand at the small of her back and the other gliding up and down between her thighs, kissing her passionately all the while, the Kansan played upon the lovely *Mexicana's* body in much the same inspired fashion that a master violinist handles his instrument.

The Latin beauty's limbs shuddered, and she took her lips from Dave Watson's, moaning as his deft touch inflamed her senses, murmuring endearments in the Spanish tongue.

The Kansan slowly brought his hand up between Consuela's legs and caused her to moan even more loudly, his middle finger still between her swollen nether lips, skimming the nub of her engorged clitoris in passing. Then up went his hand, fingers trailing throught the black, abundant muff, up over the firm and gentle swell of Consuela's belly, up over her heaving ribcage and onto her full breast, where he felt her long, thick nipple grow fully erect beneath his teasing fingers.

Dah-veed! she gasped, her hand running down over his chest and belly until it came in contact with his rod, which stood stiff as a poker.

It was the Kansan's turn to gasp as Consuela's fingers encircled his swollen sex and began to stroke it with a deftness which aroused him mightily.

She inclined her head toward him and they kissed, while she continued to manipulate the Kansan with light, yet insistent movements. Consuela proceeded to perform both of these amorous activities for several intense moments, moaning deep in her throat all the while as the Kansan continued his skillful caressing of her breasts. After some time had gone by in this manner, the *Mexicana* released her grip upon his pole and began to graze the underside of Dave's scrotum with her long fingernails.

This sent shivers up the Kansan's spine, and he felt a rising warmth in the pit of his groin, a warmth which would eventually be transformed into a raging bonfire before his pleasure had ended.

His lips still pressed firmly upon the *Mexicana's,* Dave slowly inched her body forward, until they came to the edge of his bed. And then, urging Consuela on with a gentle pressure as she cupped and fondled his testicles, the Kansan took her down upon the bed.

As his shadow covered her, the raven-haired beauty opened her legs, took hold of the Kansan's pole once more, and began to guide him into the sweet, musky place between her thighs.

Dios! she gasped as the Kansan's shaft slid into her pussy, suddenly penetrating her to its full length. She threw back her head and caught her breath, closing her eyes. And then, as the Kansan looked down upon her face, with its high-planed cheekbones and sensual, full-lipped mouth, Dave Watson saw that Consuela Delgado smiled a strange, inward smile. This smile was a revelation of dark and sensual feelings, and the Kansan was deeply moved by it, even though he did not consciously understand what it conveyed.

Slowly, ever so slowly, he began to come out of her,

until only the head of his sex was gripped by the Mexicana's throbbing cunt. And then he moved toward her once more, penetrating the gasping, dark-skinned beauty with infinite patience.

Consuela began to move and squirm beneath him, as the Kansan continued to stroke back and forth, moving in and out of her snug honeypot with slow and deliberate thrusts. Unable to stand it any longer, Consuela thrust herself at him, urging Dave to go faster.

With a sudden thrust the Kansan grunted as he butted his pelvis against the *Mexicana's,* burying his rod in her.

Dios mio! Consuela Delgado cried out into the Arizona night as her lover thrust himself deep inside her, his balls smacking lightly against her buttocks as he did. Then she arched her back beneath Dave and ground her crotch against him vigorously. The Kansan responded in kind, and they pressed against each other as a mortar is ground by a pestle. In this manner the lovers mutually stoked the fires of their passion.

Santa Maria! the Mexican beauty gasped as her orgasm broke inside her like a tidal wave over the Monterey coast. *Oh! Ooooh! Ai-i-i-i-eee!*

The Kansan's eyes went wide as she uttered those last passion-wracked cries, and he looked down at Consuela's Latin-angel face and saw that it was dark and swollen with passion. But then he had no more time to behold this awesome spectacle, for Dave Watson's own climax was upon him.

His pelvis began to jerk involuntarily as the intolerable pressure and congestion within his groin was relieved with a sudden and aching rush. What he felt brought to his mind's eye the image of molten steel being poured into a mold. And then Dave Watson cried out into the darkness of his dream, calling the name of a woman. But the name that the Kansan gave voice to was not that of Consuela Delgado, as he awakened all the Pawnees from their sleep. No, it was not the hot-blooded *Mexicana's* name at all, Dave realized as he sat up in the night, shivering and covered with sweat. The name that he had uttered belonged to Deanna Mac-Partland.

The next morning, as he rode deeper into the brown and green mass of the foothills of Colorado's Piedmont, Dave Watson shifted unesily in his saddle at the memory of what he had dreamed the night before. It was no time for thoughts of love and pleasure, the Kansan reminded himself. No, on the contrary, it was time to think of killing. . . .

Two white men watering their horses on the far side of that big hill to the east, one of the Cheyenne scouts signaled to Grey Thunder.

The warrior who led the outlaw band turned to his friend Tall Elk and spoke to him in silence.

Let us kill those two while we are here, he proposed in sign language.

The big Sioux nodded in agreement. *It is well,* he signaled back. *All white men are our enemies. Let us kill them wherever we find them.*

Grey Thunder nodded too, a grim smile on his lips. Then he turned to the braves who sat their horses behind him and nodded his head once more.

At this signal form Grey Thunder, all the Cheyennes and Sioux in the band dismounted, sliding noiselessly off the backs of their ponies, after which they proceeded to tether the animals. The attack would be made on foot, so that the braves could advance upon their quarry in silence. At this time, Grey Thunder and his Cheyennes were not interested in counting coup or other deeds of Indian valor; their immediate objective was merely to kill the two whites.

A stream meandered around the base of the big hill in question, running down into a draw on the easternmost side. This basin was formed between the base of the hill which hid the two white men and the rising ground on the stream's farther bank. The countryside in this particular section of Colorado was dotted with low hills, and the immediate visibility in any direction was, in consequence of this condition, severely limited. In contrast to the open plains, it was the perfect spot for an ambush.

The war-party consisted of twenty-nine braves, almost the full strength of Grey Thunder's outlaw band. All of them were armed with rifles and pistols, in addition to the bows and knives they always carried. Slowly the Indians fanned out, as they approached the foot of the big hill. Their leader made his way up the center of the slope, ahead of all the others, having been informed by the scout that the two unsuspecting white men were watering their horses on the exact opposite side of the hill.

The sun had barely begun to rise, and was just coming over the top of the smaller hill which stood beside, and to the northeast of, the taller one. On the far side of the hill under attack stood another small hill, which flanked it as did the other, but on the southeast. It was well into April now, and the hostiles had fled into Colorado after a series of particularly bloody raids in northwestern Kansas.

While the sun rose red and full on the far side of the big hill, Grey Thunder's band crept up under cover of shadow, since it had not yet cleared the peak. The

Cheyenne was not far from the rim of the hill, and a hard, grim smile came to his lips as he climbed in silence. He was on all fours now, his rifle held in his hand, moving with the grace and silence of a stalking bobcat. In another moment he would be at the top of the hill, where he would then be able to get the two white men on the other side within his gunsights.

On his left, no more than ten yards distant from Grey Thunder, the scout crouched just below the rim of the hill, peering over from time to time with infinite caution, making certain that the intended victims had not become aware of the presence of their attackers. He ducked back and turned toward Grey Thunder, just as the Cheyenne reached the top of the hill. The scout nodded slowly, his gesture meant to assure his leader that the white men who were watering their horses in the draw below suspected nothing.

Grey Thunder nodded back in acknowledgement of this, the hard, killer's smile still set on his lips. He rose to his knees and gently lifted his Winchester from the soil, about to peer over the hill. But he stopped suddenly and began to look from side to side, still crouching, as he paused to check the disposition of his forces.

The braves were fanned out below him on either side of his central position. The Cheyenne leader nodded as they came on, and then turned back and raised his head slowly, in order to peer over the rim of the hill.

Grey Thunder's eyes narrowed as he saw the two white men below, on the far side of the stream. They were not far from their horses, and sat on some rocks that were part of a cluster of boulders on the bank of the little rivulet. Both men faced toward the advancing hostiles, and both appeared to be in the act of cleaning their rifles; they conversed in lively tones while their mounts grazed in the grass near the bank.

Waving the other braves up the hill with a gesture meant to hasten their passage over the intervening distance, Grey Thunder turned his head and nodded at the scout, who now crouched just below the rim, his rifle at the ready. This signal indicated that he was about to share with that brave the honor of firing the first shots at the unsuspecting white men below.

The scout nodded back almost immediately, having caught Grey Thunder's meaning. He slowly raised his rifle and began to lean forward, inching his way over the rim of the hill with infinite patience as he prepared to sight down upon his prey, about to train his weapon upon the man nearest him.

Grey Thunder made his preparations as well, while the rest of the braves crept up the hill, almost at the rim now. As he leveled his Winchester, the Cheyenne's heart soared like an eagle at the thought of adding two more white scalps to his already imposing collection.

There were men among the Cheyenne who had mastered the art of eagle-catching, men who trapped, fought and conquered the great feathered chiefs of the air. Grey Thunder now felt an exhilaration which must have been akin theirs at the moment of triumph, when, after a long wait and a terrific struggle, the winged fury lay exhausted and beaten. The Cheyenne felt this triumphant elation, this wild and holy intoxication, each time that he struck down an enemy or lifted a scalp. And when he felt this, he knew to be true what he had been taught as a boy... that of all men in all the world, the Cheyenne were the greatest.

The other braves would be beside him in a moment, Grey Thunder calculated, his index finger gliding over the trigger guard as it slowly and familiarly sought the Winchester's trigger. but by the time the first of them reached the rim, he would already have shot down the white man.

He was at the very top of the hill now, kneeling as he sighted down upon his target, the rising sun imparting its red glow to the front of his body and filling his with sudden warmth as he proceeded with his work of death.

The man in Grey Thunder's sights was tall and broad-shouldered, with blond hair and a week's growth of beard that had come in a shade darker than his wavy locks. He had just put down the rag which he had used to clean his rifle, laying it beside him on the rock where he sat. His companion had also finished his gun-cleaning, and sat fondling his rifle as he stared into the limpid waters of the running stream.

Grey Thunder squinted as he peered down the length of his rifle barrel and calculated the final compensations for trajectory and windage. His finger glided onto the Winchester's trigger with reptilian smoothness and certainty. He knew that the scout would not dare to fire before he did, and so the Cheyenne took his time, relishing each moment as he made ready to bring down the blond-haired white man with a bullet aimed at the heart.

Bam! Bam! Ba-ba-bam!

A volley of shots rang out, rending the quiet fabric of the morning, their sudden noise startling the birds in the trees and grass, sending them up into the air with a frantic beating of wings as they rawked their terror and alarm in sharp, frightened voices. Nor did the roar of that volley die out at once; it continued to echo and re-echo throughout the surrounding hills.

To the consternation of the Cheyennes and their Sioux allies, not a single one of the shots fired in that long volley came from the rifles of Grey Thunder or the scout. Cries of anger and dismay went up into the air only moments after the shots had been fired, and they, too, sent their echoes out among the foothills.

These cries arose as the attacking braves watched in disbelief while Grey Thunder and the scout jerked and grunted in sudden shock as their bodies were penetrated by bullets. *The hunters had become the hunted!*

The scout's body whipped back and forth as he caught three slugs in his left side—two in the torso and one in the side of the head. His rifle went off into the air as the dying Cheyenne's finger reflexively tightened around the trigger. The impact of the slugs pitched the brave over on his right side, and he was dead by the time that his body hit the ground. His corpse rolled over the side of the hill, the rifle slipping from nerveless fingers and clattering down the rocky slope, bouncing toward the bank of the stream.

Pwop! was the sound made by the bullet that caught Grey Thunder, as it smacked into his side and glanced off his ribcage. The leader of the band of hostiles had been luckier than his scout, for that was the only bullet to hit him, although many whizzed past his head like hornets on the warpath, or threw up the soil around him, accompanied by the flat, pattering sound of their impact. But the slug that hit the Cheyenne tore through his flesh and spun him around. Grey Thunder cried out and threw his rifle up into the air, jerking his head and shoulders down suddenly as he began to pitch headlong back down the hill.

On the far side of the hill, down by the banks of the small, clear stream, the Cheyenne's intended victims jumped behind the boulders on which they had previously sat, and came up a moment later firing their rifles up at the outlaw bank for all they were worth. Their fire was reinforced by heavy volleys from each of the adjoining hills, where the first shots had originated.

As he tumbled down to the bottom of the slope, Grey Thunder realized that he had been ambushed—that someone had laid a trap for him! And a moment after he did, a series of bloodthirsty war-cries filled the air, and the Cheyenne warrior suddenly knew exactly who had perpetrated the ambush!

Pawnee! Grey Thunder told himself as he hit level ground, rolled over several times, and then staggered to his feet. *Our old enemies, the Pawnee! It is they who have done this—the white men were merely decoys!*

The shooting grew heavier, as the Cheyennes and Sioux on the rim of the hill began to return the fire of the Pawnees and their white friends. Grey Thunder heard the rapidity with which the Pawnees rained their fire upon his band, and immediately recognized the terrible sound of Spencer repeating rifles. If those Pawnees were firing Spencers, he concluded that he and his band had almost certainly been ambushed by the white chief North's scouts. The scouts were the pick of his enemies: the boldest, swiftest and deadliest of all the Pawnee warriors who ranged the Great Plains; the heavily-armed and highly disciplined braves who had proved themselves more than a match for the Cheyenne or the Sioux recently, thanks to the white man's great and deadly gift of the Spencer rifles.

Secure on his feet now, Grey Thunder looked up the slope and saw a rifle come bouncing down in the wake of a dead Sioux. Bullets whizzed through the air or whanged off the rocks, as some of the Pawnees began to concentrate their fire upon the base of the hill. As he sprinted over to pick up the fallen rifle, Grey Thunder noticed with a start that the dead body which had preceded it down belonged to his old friend, Tall Elk, the leader of the Sioux.

A quick glance at the top of the hill confirmed what the Cheyenne had already deduced. Those of his band who were still on their feet—and there were not many—now raced down the hill in full retreat. The rest of the braves lay dead or wounded, either writhing in pain or still and twisted in the grim and awkward postures of violent death. The battle was already lost, Grey Thunder told himself, firing his rifle as he backed away from the corpse of Tall Elk. It would be all that he could do to get away with his own skin.

"Flee!" he cried out to the other survivors. *"We will meet later, as planned!"*

The Cheyenne fired his rifle several times in rapid succession at the nearest hill. Once he had done this, Grey Thunder spun around and then sprinted off, the hornet-song and whine of flying bullets providing an accompaniment for his precipitate retreat. As he went, the warrior's fierce heart was gladdened by one other sound that happened to reach his ears—the cry of a dying enemy. He had shot one of the Pawnees! He had not quit the field without honor!

"Git that sum'bitch!" the Kansan cried, after he had fired the last bullet from his Henry rifle at Grey Thunder. Marcus Haverstraw had gained the top of the hill a moment earlier, and the newspaperman lay gasping beside Dave Watson, pointing at the retreating Cheyenne.

"Is that our man?" he asked, once had had caught his breath.

The Kansan dropped his Henry, and then whipped out his big Walker Colt. After he had fired off a brace of shots at Grey Thunder just before the Cheyenne disappeared behind a hill, the Kansan got to his feet and grunted by way of reply, "You're goddam right it is! That's the fella Soaring Hawk pointed out to me. That's the boy what's got Deanna MacPartland!"

On the hill to Dave's right, Soaring Hawk jumped up and waved his Spencer over his head, whooping shrilly. The Pawnees on both hills had risen to their feet now, still firing down upon the retreating hostiles as they screeched their fearsome and triumphant war-cries.

Grey Thunder had a momentary respite, hidden from sight as he now was from the devastating Spencers of his Pawnee foes. Behind him came three of the six Cheyennes and Sioux who had fled the scene; the other three lay upon the hard, Colorado earth in pools of their own blood.

"To the horses!" Grey Thunder said in a strangled voice, waving the pitiful remainder of his band on as he staggered toward the waiting horses and the men who had stayed behind to guard them.

"Many scalps!" cried Soaring Hawk in a voice that was shot through with triumph and savage exultation. *"Today the Pawnee will take many scalps from their defeated enemies!"*

"All but the one I'm hankerin' after," the Kansan muttered as he sped down the hill in hot pursuit of Grey Thunder. And behind him, gun in hand, and puffing like a Southern Pacific engine running out of steam in the Rocky Mountains, Marcus P. Haverstraw stumbled, gun in hand, down the slope after his saddlemate.

"Wait for me," he panted, but the Kansan never heard him. Dave Watson was too far ahead of the newspaperman now, and he was totally absorbed in the pursuit of the warrior who had taken Deanna MacPartland. A moment later he disappeared from sight, going behind the same hill which had served as the Cheyenne's cover only seconds before.

Boom! Bam! Blambam!

Four shots rang out, loud and clear, from the place

where Dave Watson had just gone.

"Oh, Godfrey!" Marcus cried out in sudden alarm, raising his pistol and running over to the side of the hill. When he reached the spot where the Kansan had disappeared, the newspaperman ducked down, raised his pistol, and slowly peered around the mass of grass, earth and stones that was the profile of the hill. What he saw next caused the Connecticut journalist's eyes to widen and his jaw to drop open to the limits of its hinges.

The Kansan lay flat on his back upon the ground, not five feet from where Marcus Haverstraw peered around the side of the hill. And ten feet in front of Dave Watson's body, a Cheyenne brave lay face-down upon the ground, a pool of blood forming beneath his chest.

"David Lee!" the reporter cried, going over to the Kansan's side and falling down to his knees. "Are you all right?" he asked hesitantly.

His eyes went wide as he saw blood trickle down from the left side of the Kansan's head. For a moment the stupefied newspaperman took him for dead, but Dave Watson moaned suddenly and blinked open his eyes.

"What the Sam Hill you doin' here?" he croaked, not expecting to see his friend.

"You, ah, just had a little altercation with a Cheyenne," Marcus told him as a number of Pawnees dashed past them. "He's, ah, laying over there."

"Sum'bitch was like to take me when I come 'round the bend," Dave told the newspaperman, reaching out and grabbing his shoulder with one hand as he attempted to pull himself up to a sitting position. But then he winced, groaned, and lay back down upon the ground, his free hand going up to the wound on the side of his head.

"Just relax for a minute, old man," cautioned Marcus. "You've been shot, you know." As Dave lowered his bloodstained hand, the reporter peered at the Kansan's temple. "Luckily, it appears to be little more than a flesh wound," he murmured.

"How's the Cheyenne doin'?" the Kansan asked through clenched teeth.

"I believe he's howled his last war-whoop," Marcus answered, reaching down as he helped Dave to a sitting position. "You popped him in the chest, it appears—twice, judging from the holes in his back. He's down for the count."

"Is that . . . Grey Thunder?" Marcus asked after a long silence.

After squinting at the corpse of the fallen Cheyenne for some time, the Kansan shook his head, stopping an instant later to moan and press his hands to his temples.

"No, that ain't him," he grunted in pain as the blood from his wound began to flow again. "This sucker laid in wait fer me, whilst Grey Thunder an' them other bucks done hightailed it outta here."

"Well, the Pawnees were hot on his trail, if that's any consolation," Marcus told him.

"It'll be a consolation if Soaring Hawk or one of them Pawnee scouts comes back here carryin' that sum'bitch's scalp," the Kansan muttered darkly, puffing and grunting as he struggled to rise to his feet.

"Well, let's hope for the best," said Marcus Haverstraw, ever the optimist. But when the Pawnees returned, the two men were to be disappointed.

"Grey Thunder too fast," Soaring Hawk told them in English. "He ride away before we catch him."

"His pony is truly swift," Red-Armed Panther informed the Kansan in Pawnee. "He will not be brought down today, nor will the two braves who rode off behind him."

"Well, I reckon that'll just have to do fer today," the Kansan muttered as he bent over to pick up his Walker Colt from the rocky ground. "But I ain't finished with that sucker yet." His eyes were hard and cold as he straightened up. "I owe ol' Grey Thunder a bullet or two. An' I aim to pay my debt soon as possible." He nodded his head and smiled a tight, bitter smile.

"We'll meet again," he said, turning to Marcus Haverstraw. "An' when we do, I'll see that Cheyenne sum'bitch gits ever'thin' I'm savin' fer him!"

Soaring Hawk nodded at this, a fierce smile upon his lips. "That is good, my brother," he said in a low, even voice. "That means we will take more Cheyenne scalps." The Pawnee's smile was terrible to behold.

He turned to the Pawnee scouts and spoke to them in their own tongue. They listened and then voiced their own thoughts to him once he had finished, each man with the same fierce gleam in his eye as Soaring Hawk. "We have good times," the Pawnee told his white blood-brother after he had heard the scouts. "We catch up with Grey Thunder plenty soon . . . and then we kill heap many Cheyenne."

When Duncan Stearns and his sixty riders came upon Grey Thunder's hidden camp, he learned that only two braves had been left behind to guard it. The only other occupants of the site were five Cheyenne women, several small children . . . and Deanna Mac-Partland.

The big Scotsman had enlisted the aid of two Crow scouts, and they had soon been able to pick up Grey

Thunder's trail, a trail of death and destruction which had led to the foothills of Colorado. It was almost noon, and the sun was high in the blue, cloudless sky when the riders caught sight of the Indian camp. By the limited activity displayed there, the Crows concluded that the main body of hostiles had left the camp. But for safety's sake, the scouts recommended that it be taken by stealth.

"We're going to surround that camp, gentlemen," Stearns told his men as he pointed down from his vantage point on one of the hills which overlooked it. "We'll dismount here, leaving our horses at the base of this hill. Ten of our party will remain with the horses on the off-chance that any of those red devils should happen to return home."

Saying this, the redheaded giant turned his head slowly, his glance flickering from face to face as he looked over the men who had followed him from Hays City on his quest for blood and vengeance. Stearns looked over the assemblage carefully, deciding who among the riders would go and who would stay behind with the horses.

His hired killers would be in the vanguard of the advance, Stearns decided; they would be with him to a man. After the few remaining warriors who had been left behind to guard the hostile camp had been killed off, the next targets would be the Cheyenne women and children. And then there was the question of scalps. . . .

It was Duncan Stearn's intention to lift every scalp in the camp which grew black hair on it, regardless of the sex or age of its possessor. If the ranchers, townsmen and settlers whom he had persuaded to join the expedition happened not to be squeamish about gunning down Indian women and children, the Scotsman doubted that many of them would have the stomach for scalping their victims. That was where his boys would come in.

He proceeded to point out those men he deemed least likely to actively participate in a massacre, instructing them to guard the horses, weapons in hand, while he and the remainder of the force proceeded on foot to surround the Cheyenne encampment.

"The white woman is down there, gentlemen," Stearns told the riders, "the woman who was stolen from my ranch outside Hays City. I have been actively seeking her return ever since that time, for I had vowed that Miss MacPartland should not languish in durance vile while there was life in this body of mine. I cannot tolerate the thought that so fair a flower, so lovely a specimen of white womanhood, should have to serve as slave to the Indian beast."

Here he paused and looked over his forces once more, a steely glint now in his cold eyes.

"I vowed that this young woman would be restored to her people—to the civilization which had nourished and elevated her, the civilization which is her birthright. She is a white woman, gentlemen—a defenseless maiden who has been abducted. . . ." He lowered his voice and frowned. ". . . and God only knows what else." With a sudden creak of leather, Duncan Stearns shifted his weight in the saddle. "Our scouts inform me that she is dressed in squaw's clothing, so be especially careful as we go in. I want her unharmed." His icy blue eyes fell upon the faces of the riders once more. "Her name is Miss MacPartland. Please treat her with all due respect."

His face took on a stern and righteous look. "Those savages must not go unpunished," he told the men after a long silence, in which he turned his head to gaze down once more upon Grey Thunder's camp. Then, patting the Colt .45 in his holster, Stearns turned back to face the riders. "You know what to do, gentlemen," Stearns went on, scanning the faces of his listeners. "Let's teach the red dogs a lesson they'll never forget. Let's teach them never to meddle with white men again."

The men growled and muttered their agreement, stirring restlessly in their saddles.

"Prepare your weapons, gentlemen," the big redhead grunted as he swung out of his saddle. "The time has come to use them."

Once dismounted, he turned to his right-hand man, the killer known as Crawford.

"You know what to do," he said in a low, tense voice as the scar-faced desperado got off his horse.

"I shorely do, Mister Stearns," the murderer replied amiably. "I shorely do."

"Miss MacPartland must not be harmed in any way," the Scotsman went on, in a voice meant only for Crawford's ears. "But all Indians are fair game. I want every Indian scalp in the camp."

Crawford nodded, a pleasant smile upon his face. "Now, don't you worry none, Mister Stearns. Me'n the boys'll take care of ever'thin' right nice."

"Make sure that you do." Duncan Stearns growled back at the man, just before he turned away to look down at the Cheyenne camp one last time.

As he raced through the foothills, the war-cries of the victorious Pawnees still rang and re-echoed in Grey Thunder's memory, filling the Cheyenne's heart with a burning shame. And even though he had escaped the deadly trap which his old enemies had cleverly set for him, the warrior burned as he realized what the Pawnees had done.

They had used the two white men as decoys, in order to lure him and the members of his band into an ambush, one which had been so successful that only Grey Thunder and two other braves had managed to escape with their lives. He knew that for a fact; the Plains Indians did not believe in taking prisoners.

The ambush had been so carefully laid that even his shrewd and battle-hardened Cheyenne scouts did not catch wind of it and uncover any of the Pawnees' traces. It was unthinkable to Grey Thunder that any Indian would stoop so low as to bait a trap with the connivance of white men. His gorge rose at the very thought. But the Pawnees were the dogs of the white men, the Cheyenne told himself as his pony galloped into the gathering darkness. They were base enough to resort to such a dishonorable trick. They had forfeited the right to be called warriors—to be called men!

Shame was swept away by fury, as Grey Thunder rode on into the night, his rage mounting as he imagined the victory songs and dances that the Pawnees must be performing around their campfire. And he could hear them barking their triumph into the night sky, like dogs baying at the full moon.

Grey Thunder has been defeated by the Pawnee!
All his warriors lie dead in the dust!
The Sioux who rode with him are all dead and lying in the dust!
Grey Thunder has run from the Pawnee in the manner of a Cheyenne maid fleeing the presence of a young man!
Grey Thunder's band will ride no more, for the Pawnee have laid low their ancient enemies, the Cheyenne!
Grey Thunder has been defeated!

As fury supplanted shame in the Cheyenne's heart, so did horror replace fury when he arrived at his campsite and beheld, by the cold light of the moon, the results of the massacre.

The moment he caught sight of the despoiled camp, Grey Thunder caught his breath and immediately slowed his pony to a walk. But he kept on, never stopping, even as the nightmare of horror and desolation greeted his eyes everywhere he looked, assaulting him with an almost palpable force, causing even that battle-hardened warrior to gag and nearly pitch sidewise off the back of his mount. But he never stopped, not for a moment, and continued on his grim way to the spot where the kites were feasting beneath the dead moon on the carceasses of slaughtered Cheyenne women and children.

The enemy was long gone: Grey Thunder felt that in his bones as he rode through the remains of his camp. But even if the enemy had been present in full strength, he would have proceeded. He would have begun to chant his death-song, charging at full-tilt, knowing well that the headlong rush would be his last. At that moment, he did not want to live.

But this was not to be, for the enemy was nowhere to be found. Grey Thunder rode in silence as he walked his pony through that place of death and desolation, tears streaming from his dark and anguished eyes. *Women dead, children dead; all scalped.* He groaned, but it caught in his dry and constricted throat as he rode over the killing ground, whose very soil was soaked with the blood of atrocity.

An Indian would not do such a thing, Grey Thunder told himself as he dismounted and walked among the mutilated corpses whose eyes had already been plucked out by the carrion birds who wheeled overhead, rawking and scolding, impatient for him to depart, so that they could resume their grim work.

Not even those dogs of Pawnees, debased as they were, would stoop to such a thing, Grey Thunder concluded, rage and sorrow filling his heart as he lifted the tattered and bloodstained flap of his teepee and entered within. He stood with the flap held open, blinking as his eyes slowly adjusted to the gloom. No, only the white men would have done such a deed—such a dreadful thing as the scalping and mutilation of defenseless women and children. It would have been enough to kill the two warriors who had guarded the camp, Grey Thunder told himself, horror numbing his feelings; but the deaths of the Cheyenne's brother, Running Antelope, and the brave named Burning Grass had not been enough to appease the bloodthirsty attackers.

Tears streamed down the fierce warrior's cheeks as he came out of the tent, his feelings suddenly returning with all the violence of a swollen river overflowing its banks. *The great atrocity had been committed by white men: He had absolutely no doubt about that. And they had taken Golden Woman from him, as well.*

There was much to do, Grey Thunder told himself as he rode away from that place of horror and shame. He would be revenged upon the Pawnee for he knew that they were the same braves who served as scouts with the white chief, North. He would be revenged upon them all. He remembered the faces of the two whites who had served to decoy him and his warriors into that deadly ambush. If he ever chanced upon them again, he would promptly settle the score with a terrible vengeance.

And the whites who had taken Golden Woman from him?

Grey Thunder gritted his teeth, looking back one more time at the remains of his camp, at whose far end the kites had already begun to swoop down again upon the mutilated bodies. It was to be total war, he decided. He would learn to be as vicious and deceitful as the whites. He would raise the tribes and wage war upon them all.

The moon shone down upon the foothills with a cold light, covering everything that it touched with a patina of silver. Grey Thunder looked up into the night sky and swore by Maijun, the Great Spirit of his people, that he would not rest until he had found Golden Woman, then he would again claim her as his own. No other man would possess her . . . not while the Cheyenne lived.

There was much to do, Grey Thunder told himself as he rode off into the night, his heart bursting with its dreadful freight of grief and rage. *There would be much killing when the summer came. And in a short time, the plains would be awash in blood.*

The following morning the Pawnees rode into Grey Thunder's camp, with Dave Watson and Marcus Haverstraw at their head, flanking Soaring Hawk. They said not a word until they had all dismounted and surveyed the awful carnage and desolation. The first man to speak was the Kansan's blood-brother.

"Those who came before," he said in a low voice, turning his face to Dave Watson, "not Indian." An expression of anger commingled with disgust came onto his face. "White man do this," he said bitterly. "White man kill Cheyenne women and children, and then scalp 'em."

"Who could have done such a dreadful thing?"

asked a horrified Marcus Haverstraw.

"I 'spect we'll find out right soon, once't we git back to Hays City," Dave Watson told him, looking past the devastated camp of Grey Thunder, toward the state of Kansas.

"What about Deanna MacPartland?" the reporter asked, a look of concern upon his angular face.

"I reckon the same fella what laid waste to this here camp done took Deanna with 'im." The Kansan's eyes were as cold as death, as he nodded slowly and patted his holstered Walker Colt. "I aim to look that fella up . . . right soon."